LILIANE'S
BALCONY

Advance Praise for *Liliane's Balcony*

"In *Liliane's Balcony*, Kelcey Parker skillfully interweaves the voices of a wide range of richly drawn characters, each experiencing Fallingwater in diverse, compelling ways. For anyone who has visited, the vivid descriptions will take you back; for anyone who has not experienced Fallingwater first-hand, this book will conjure the magic out of thin air. But while Fallingwater is at the center of this swirling drama, *Liliane's Balcony* is at its heart a tale of love—the struggle to imagine it, the struggle to find it, and the struggle to keep it."

—JIM DANIELS, author of *Birth Marks*

"*Liliane's Balcony* proves stylishly and poignantly that just as buildings don't have to be huge to be architecturally daring, narratives don't have to be massive in scale to be grand in accomplishment. The story lines here—a contemporary one set on a tour of Fallingwater, a historical one featuring the original owner, the venturesome, conflicted, and fascinating Liliane—are ingeniously designed and expertly joined. The result is a meditation on marriage, architecture, womanhood, ghosts, and the idea of the *genius loci* that will linger with the reader long after the book is closed. This reminded me of great novels of architecture and psychology like Kathryn Davis's *Hell* and Joanna Scott's *The Manikin*, but Kelcey Parker is a unique talent, and *Liliane's Balcony* is a revelation."

—MICHAEL GRIFFITH, author of *Trophy*

LILIANE'S

A NOVELLA OF FALLINGWATER

BALCONY

BY KELCEY PARKER

Rose Metal Press

2013

Rose Metal Press, Inc.
P.O. Box 1956
Brookline, MA 02446
rosemetalpress@gmail.com
www.rosemetalpress.com

Library of Congress Control Number: 2013944890
ISBN: 978-0-9887645-3-8

Cover and interior design by Heather Butterfield

Cover art: *Lady by the Pond*, by Fran Forman
More information and artwork can be viewed on the artist's website: www.franforman.com

Publisher's Note: This is a work of fiction, part of which is based on real events.

The song lyrics listed in the Amanda sections are from "Go Your Own Way," written by Lindsey Buckingham, performed by Fleetwood Mac on the 1977 album *Rumours*, released by Warner Bros. Records. (Note: Some quotes are intentionally incorrect interpretations of the lyrics.)

The song lyrics listed on page 114 are from "It's the End of the World as We Know It (And I Feel Fine)," written by R.E.M. and recorded on the 1987 album *Document*, released by I.R.S. Records.

A full list of sources can be found on page 201.

This book is manufactured in the United States of America and printed on acid-free paper.

For my mother, Janice Bobrovcan,
who shares a birthday with Liliane

All artists occasionally put something outrageous in their works to get them noticed—signature pieces that guarantee their creators a *succès de scandale*. For Gertrude Stein it was deadening repetition, for Frank Gehry it has been undulating curves and titanium, for Picasso the distorted human forms in his *Demoiselles d'Avignon* and *Guernica*. In Fallingwater, I see two such signature pieces: the illusion of water coursing through the house, and Liliane's oversailing balcony.

FRANKLIN TOKER,
FALLINGWATER RISING

Which is almost as provocative as the story of the ghost, the one that is said to haunt Fallingwater's master bedroom. She is allegedly a woman in a white nightgown staring out the window. She never speaks, just looks sadly at the falls.

KEVIN GRAY,
"MODERN GOTHIC"

Prologue

LILIANE

Liliane strains to hear the falling water. She closes her eyes to open her ears to hear the water falling, for that is the point of the house, the architect had explained, to live with the waterfall. It was too plain merely to see the waterfall. One had to live with it, hear its voice, feel its pulse. But Liliane, in her bed, in early September, with the terrace door open despite the threat and scream of late-summer insects, cannot. She opens her ears wider but no waterfall. Insects. Ting ting of dishes downstairs. No waterfall.

And what of Stoops? Must one hear Stoops? Must one live with Stoops?

Grace. Grace is the name Liliane's husband calls Stoops. Grace is across the world in California, but Liliane can hear her. Liliane can hear young Stoops Goldilocksing through the rooms of the California house, claiming what's not hers. Liliane doesn't care a whit about the commissioned California house, which, all glass and chrome, is like an oversized display case at the department store. (No wonder her husband likes it so.) But a stooping nurse? Liliane hears her so clearly she wonders if Stoops is here now. It is easy enough to hide someone away at Bear Run. Liliane hardly recalls where all the servants scurry off to at night. Not that Stoops would stoop to servants' quarters; Stoops would stow herself away in the husband's room. Liliane winces, takes another pill for her pain.

Stoops handles her husband's pain. "Where does it hurt, Mr. K? Here? Is that better?" Liliane hears Stoops nursing her husband, hears her husband say, "Yes, Grace, there, yes." Liliane hears the first time Stoops calls him by his first name, hears the silence that follows, hears the knowing smiles.

The sounds are too much. Liliane is supposed to live with the waterfall, not with Stoops. She lifts herself to a sitting position and plants her feet on the floor until the room stops Stooping. Stop. Another pill. A drink of water. The pill and the water fall together through her throat. She clutches the edge of the nightstand to pull herself up. Her body sways like a late-summer cattail in a gentle wind. Steadied, Liliane clasps the door's latch and steps onto her balcony.

She must have floated across the stony platform. How else could she be here at its edge, so far from the door she thought she was still clutching, leaning her torso over the low parapet to hear the waterfall. And there, below her, not so much like an old friend (of which she has many) but a best friend (of which she has none), yes, there it is: a moving surface, a moonlit triangle, hypotenused by the rock's edge. That edge marks the point of transformation from stream to spray, from slipsong to scream. *Schäumt er unmutig / Stufenweise / Zum Abgrund.* She can hear Goethe's words, Schubert's chorus, but she can't hear it, the water. Darkness covers sight, not sound, yes? She looks up, away from the silent water, and hears the sharp whistle of a hawk perched somewhere in the surrounding fortress of trees, upside-down brooms that sweep the sky.

The sky is a constellation of pain pills. Liliane reaches out her hand and squeezes a cluster into her fist. She puts one in her mouth, swallows it, and thinks of water. Where is the voice?

The architect had strutted about the house as it neared completion, and, with the workers adding to the audience, pointed with his cane to this feature and that, informing them of each detail and design function. The one that always stuck with Liliane, that she experienced more deeply as the years passed, was the relationship between outside and inside. The inside's floors and walls are made of rough outdoor stone, quarried just downstream, and the rock of the fireplace (strange to remember how it was once outside, how they used to picnic on it) could not be contained; it spills into the main room. The "basement" is the stream itself. The low ceilings, the architect had said, create a feeling of protection and comfort from the outdoors, while the overhanging terraces can only be compared, he declared, to the cliffs of the Romantic sublime. (*Ragen Klippen!*) How he proclaimed about his design. Would anyone tolerate a painter who explained his own paintings so? She forgave him because he'd been right about all of it. Yes, she'd quibbled with him over the lighting, a few pieces of furniture, a rug here and there; it was her house, after all. Still, she wanted to tell him: *Don't you know? The house speaks for itself.*

But its language was not language at all. Music, perhaps, chords of concrete, stone, glass; the melody: falling water.

She nonetheless understood his need to define the house for the workers, the press, the visitors—those who had to absorb its details quickly, those who could not live with the waterfall but only admire the house floating above it. Over the years she would pause to consider the fact that she and her husband and son were the only ones in the world who experienced the house as a house. The servants experienced it as a workplace. Visitors experienced it as temporary guests; photographers as photographers; scholars as scholars. She experienced it weekend after weekend as home.

After the scaffolding was removed and the house was complete, Liliane could imagine that it had simply grown up from the water's edge like a living thing, like one of her rare orchids back at Fox Chapel. Her husband preferred to think in terms of violence, of the rumble of rocks at a fault line. (As if an earthquake does anything but destroy.) The architect said: *Think of a bird's nest. Organic order,* he said, *dramatic refuge.*

She is at the farthest edge of the house. Her white linen gown flaps in the wind, and a September chill reaches up and grabs her legs. One question she has always pondered: if one is on the balcony, is one inside or outside? The breeze says outside. But the balcony is not an exposed rock's edge; it's part of the house, designed by the architect. Behind her is her room, its warm glow. The French doors are open and the light spills onto the stone patterned ground. The architect had been so clever at dissolving the boundaries of the two.

But what, she would like to know, does one do when there is a Stoop at the entrance to a house? When a very prominent Stoop divides the indoors from the outdoors? Is there an architectural solution to that? She hears a bullfrog, but no answer, no waterfall. It is the contrast between inside and outside that she can no longer abide. Her inside, her outside. Outside, she is the proud Mrs. K—, who owns a department store, travels the world, patronizes the arts, and rules over the famous house. Inside she is withered, neglected, scorned.

Even when she returns to Pittsburgh, attends board meetings, assesses inventory, and sleeps in the downtown flat, she hears the white noise of the waterfall. Is that what the architect meant when he said you will live with the waterfall? Had he meant it will never leave you, no matter where you go? *Des Menschen Seele / Gleicht dem Wasser: / Vom Himmel kommt es, / Zum Himmel steigt es, / Und wieder nieder / Zur Erde muß es, / Ewig wechselnd.* Where has it gone?

The cantilevered balcony stirs and settles, presses an indiscernible measure heavier on the living room below. Liliane knows that gravity will get the better of it someday; it will Stoop. Even houses such as this are not immortal. She plucks another pain pill from the sky.

You will live with the waterfall, the architect had said.

At last, at last—as if someone has switched on the amplifiers—she hears its familiar voice cry out to her.

And die with me, the waterfall says.

One

JANIE

Janie has recently begun referring to her husband as *the man*: The man is in my bed. The man is at work. The man is sitting across from me at Cracker Barrel. She doesn't call him the man to his face, but she has stopped speaking his name and is waiting to see if he will notice.

"God, it's ugly," says the man.

How can he tell? They are headed toward the House and she can hear but not see it. It hadn't occurred to her that she would hear it first, but she hears it, the rush of the water. It's beautiful to her not so much like a song, but like an orchestra tuning in the pit. The tour group is crunching along the path beside a retaining wall lined with the tight white fists of rhododendron buds. The House becomes visible now through the woods and Janie discerns, through the vertical lines of trees, long planes of concrete stacked like multiple horizons. She responds to the man's comment with one of the expressions she makes in her cubicle when the person on the other end of the phone cannot see her.

"What?" he says. "Look at it."

Isn't ugly or beautiful beside the point? Still, it is not the view she expected to see. She expected her first sight of the House to be from the only angle she's ever seen, the one in all the photos, the one that looks up to the House set majestically on its waterfall pedestal. And here she is above the House, walking down toward it, no waterfall in sight. Everything the wrong direction, just like her life.

The trees form a mottled canopy of sunlight and green, and they follow the path and the sound to the small bridge where they were instructed to stop and wait for their guide. The group's willingness to follow instructions makes Janie want to do just the opposite, whatever that might be, but the House renders her into submission. Its lines reach toward her then recede, and its beige horizontal walls bask in bright sun then fold sharply into shadow, like origami. It surrounds with the sound of the water.

A portly man appears and introduces himself as the guide. He walks the group halfway across the small bridge and pauses. He rattles off more rules they are expected to follow, and a young girl is the only one in the group with the sense to protest. The water forms a pool under the House and Janie can see its far edge, which must form the waterfall of the picture, low-edged layers of balcony jutting above like cliffs.

Janie swats at a small cloud of gnats. *Christ*, she thinks, *this is no place for a baby.*

"I'm sure it's nice on the inside," the man draws her close and whispers, "but the outside looks like math class."

The man thinks that just because he has some new gray hairs he is wise.

AMANDA

There's a song going through Amanda's head. She can't remember the words or the name of the song, but she suspects it is by Fleetwood Mac. The tour guide stops them before the footbridge to introduce himself. Arthur. She can hardly hear him over the noise of the water. He is the Wizard of Oz, the one after Toto has pulled back the curtain. Arthur floats in and out of first person singular and plural. "I'd like to welcome you here on this beautiful day. We are delighted to share this very special place with you. You have chosen one of my favorite times of year because, as you can see, we are almost in full bloom this weekend. The rhododendrons blossom every Fourth of July, and we like to say that we are snowing in summer. I'm going to tell you a bit about us. We were built from 1936 to 1939..."

What's this we shit? she is thinking. She is thinking of her dad, of her dead dad, of this phrase of his, of that teasing in his eyes when he said it, of how amazing he would think this place is and how it would feel if she could stand beside him, if she could hear him conclude his familiar expression: *Do you have a frog in your pocket?*

(She is certain she hears a frog at that very moment. Dad?)

A preteen in the group has some sort of conniption, and Amanda enters the House trying to net the song darting through her head like a butterfly because her dad hurts too much. He always comes out of nowhere like that. Doesn't she have enough to worry about? Like what day it is? Like what the hell she's doing here? Alone?

But not alone. What is so alone about being in a group, is one way to look at it. And with a guide. Arthur says we are the most visited home in the world; Arthur says our reinforced concrete had to be reinforced a few years ago; Arthur says we are led through the deliberately small stoop of the entrance into the expansive open floor plan; Arthur says we are to show our receipts to the woman at the desk as we enter. Amanda's arm brushes against the leather jacket of a motorcycle man as they negotiate who goes first through the small entrance. He appears to be alone too.

She is lured within as if by the song of Sirens, and the sound of the waterfall fills the main room even more than the light that pours through the walls of windows. She blinks her eyes to adjust from the darkness of the entry to the light shining in.

The flat plane of the floor is parallel to the low plane of the ceiling, and everything is panorama, look left, look straight, look out, look right, look, look. She is inside a giant's eyeball with the lids nearly closed, like the giant is dozing and dreaming. Like she has crawled through its ear and is roaming around in its dream world.

Arthur leads the group past another group gathered by the fireplace. It pleases Amanda the way total strangers can come together in agreement over a set of rules. Then it's like they're not strangers but teammates, comrades. But everyone is so hush-hush and solemn, like they're in church, like the tour guides are giving the Mass, even though the House is alive and is the opposite of church. Or is what church should be. Amanda would like to raise her hand and suggest that they crack open some bourbon and beer and have a proper party. Wouldn't it be interesting to talk to one another and find out why they're all here at this very moment? To dispel with the obvious—fate, chance, itineraries—but then she'd have to confess that she doesn't even know why she herself is here. And she can imagine how her party would go: cold beer, straight bourbon, a dozen strangers sharing tales of what it means to be human, and she would say, *If I could, baby, I'd give you my world*. There! The words to the song! *You can call it another lonely day*.

Moments later they are escorted onto a large flat balcony with a Buddha head. Amanda steadies herself on this giant's spatula, ready to be flipped.

THE DAUGHTER

The daughter can feel the ghosts.

JANIE

On the balcony, supported by, from what she can tell, nothing, Janie thinks of Emerson, his transparent eyeball. This must be something of what he meant, something about Universal Currents or Universal Being and currents flowing through. She'll have to reread it. But she remembers the bit about the eyeball and seeing all, being nothing. Over the balcony's edge is the waterfall, and she definitely feels like nothing, just a being who sees water, trees, rocks. Is her body failing her? The man has said so. The doctors have said so. If she could be bodiless, she wouldn't have to worry about such questions or their answers. She could just explore Emerson's pure idea.

And maybe that could help explain the omnipresence of Yogi Bear and sign after sign for Jellystone Park that they passed on their way here.

"They should call it Yogi Bear Run," the man had said as they drove to the House. He was pushing the seek button of the rental car's radio. There weren't any stations, just a lot of fuzz.

Janie had kept her finger on the clicker of the window. She pressed one side, then the other, and her window went up and down, up and down. The hot wind blew in, stopped, blew in, stopped, and she was in control.

"You know, instead of Bear Run," the man explained.

Up ahead was a man on a motorcycle. All Janie could see of his body were his arms stretched up to the handlebars. They crested a country hill and the whole world was scattered barns and rolling mountains. As they descended, the view was closed up and the air was cooled down by tall pines. A bear carved from a tree trunk stood at the road's edge, growling mutely like God. At least it wasn't Yogi.

They'd stopped at an intersection behind the motorcycle, white and gleaming as if it were cleaned by a dentist. The motorcycle said Harley-Davidson in several places, and the rider's jacket said it once. The Harley turned left and from the side with his arms and legs extended, the rider looked like a terrified cat with its claws caught on a wall.

The man beside her said, "Check your cell phone and see if we get any reception out in these boonies."

Janie hoped they did not get reception; she did not want anyone to call today. They would call soon enough.

JOSIAH QUIMBY

Josiah Quimby is a man of high culture and Harley-Davidsons. He is headed out on the highway looking for adventure in the form of American history and/or modern architecture just off the Pennsylvania Turnpike. All he needs is a hot shower at a Motel 6, and he'll be off again. He sees Hershey bars and Gettysburg in his future. That's because Josiah Quimby's future is inextricably intertwined with the past. His family goes all the way the hell back to the Mayflower, and you better believe he's proud of the country started by his kin. Did your kin start a country? Not to mention the number one country in the planetary system? Didn't think so.

Plus it gives him a chance to ride his hog through the rolling highlands, where there's not quite so many damn semis on his ass. So there he was in the parking lot, revving his engine a few more times in protest of the entry fee. That's a tank of gas right there. And for what, a house tour? He never would understand rich people. But no way was Josiah Quimby going to let that lady in the booth or the car behind him see him turn his bike around over the double-digit cost. He would prove to Little-Miss-Twenty-Dollars-Did-I-See-You-Wince? that he did not in fact wince, that he had cashola to spare when it came to famous architects and houses built on water.

Water*falls*, not water. Damn. He still had it in his head that the house was built on water, ever since Rini said, "Are you going to that house built on water?" And Josiah had said yes because if there was a house built on water you better believe he was going to go see it, and because he didn't like her thinking she knew more than he did about important places in America. Especially since she had said to him: "I thought you'd be a whole lot taller when you stood up."

You think you've met every last person in your head, neck, and shoulder of the woods, and then one night at Coop's there's teeny Rini sitting at the bar next to an empty stool. Josiah had regaled her with his plans to hop on his hog for the Fourth of July and celebrate the country founded by his kinfolk. Rini seemed duly impressed about the Mayflower, and Josiah got it in his mind to kiss her on the lips before that first night was over. After an hour or so of scintillating conversation, Josiah got up to use the facilities. When he returned and caught sight of her figure facing the bar, he paused a moment to take in the beauty of her gently curved silhouette backlit by the bar light, and observed that the fluttery sleeve of her blouse rather reminded him of a waterfall as it fell from her shoulder. Feeling like a prince who has stumbled upon a sleeping princess, he positioned himself behind her, aligned his head with hers, and pressed his lips against her leathersoft cheek. Having just returned from the restroom, Josiah Quimby thought he might piss his pants.

He reclaimed his seat beside her and they sat that way, side-by-side facing the wall of liquor bottles, for some time. Josiah concentrated on taking swigs of his beer at different times than Rini did. When he couldn't stand it another damn minute that this woman had not acknowledged his gentleman's kiss, that's when she said the thing about thinking he'd be taller.

And what do you think he did? He clutched that woman's head between his hands and kissed her lips just like he'd had the notion to do before.

THE DAUGHTER

Maybe not here on the balcony, but definitely in the house. But is it just one ghost or many ghosts? And why can't they learn interesting words in Spanish class, like ghost or ghosts? Who cares about *gato* or *gatos*? *Mesa* or *mesas*? Although it's hard to think of *casa* the same after you've been in this *casa*. It's like a horizontal Jenga tower! *Como se dice haunted house?* She wants to ask the pudgy tour guide Artie that question just to see what he'd say. She knows he knows about the ghost or ghosts, and she's pretty sure he doesn't know a syllable of *Español*, so it would be fun to watch him try to take a swing at that knuckleball.

But two minutes into the tour, before they even got in the house, Mom had already given her the Eye, the old *Ojo No-No*, because when Artie pulled out a notecard, held up a finger, and read off the dos and do nots like a kindergarten teacher on the first day of school, the daughter, thinking him *muy ridiculoso*, had snickered aloud. When she saw her mom's look, she turned the snicker into a catch in the throat, which turned into a violent cough, complete with pounding of fist on sternum, apologies to the crowd, further coughs, more apologies, and, when she felt her mom's grip tighten around the back of her neck, an instant end to the violent attack. Dad stood with his arms across his chest and winked at her.

AMANDA

So maybe she does know why she's here and he goes by the name of Motherfucker. But that spurious tale wouldn't go over so hot at a party now would it? *Tell me why,* Amanda wants to ask Arthur who seems to know everything, *everything turned around.*

They return from the balcony to the living room and Arthur explains that even the couch is a cantilever. Arthur says how much the Kaufmann family liked to entertain, noting that there are extra tables that add on to the main dining table, seating up to sixteen guests. "And if you look down at your feet you will see the rugs that were chosen by Mrs. K—." He says that Mrs. K— thought the ones the famous architect selected were too formal. "And so you see that she got her way."

Amanda wonders about Mrs. K—'s parties. Once everyone felt comfortable on the cantilevered couches and animal fur rugs, did they reach into their chests, remove their hearts, and hold them out for others to see? And if so, whose was the blackest? Whose trembled and cried?

Open up, Amanda thinks when Arthur directs everyone's attention to a glass casing, which he pulls open. It leads to a staircase that goes straight down to the waterfall. The hatch, he calls it. *Everything's waiting for you.*

THE DAUGHTER

Holy wow. Stairs to a waterfall?

She catches the ponytail man looking at her and realizes her mouth is open and that her face must look like a cuckoo clock. He smiles at her, so she closes her mouth and sneers with menace.

That settles it, though. She is going to be an architect, and she is going to design haunted houses with staircases that lead to wherever she decides. Down into a pig pen, or up to a bird's nest. To the end of the rainbow. To a candy factory. To a ghost's grave.

JANIE

Why does she suddenly feel like an egg that has traveled through a Fallopian tube and arrived in a uterus? Something about the narrow entrance, the open room, the water, the white noise of a womb, her empty womb.

JOSIAH QUIMBY

The tour guide directs the group's attention to a portrait of the man who commissioned the famous architect to build the House. Josiah Quimby studies the image. A little preppy with the sweater vest and walking stick, but a man's man for sure. An idea is formulating in Josiah Quimby's mind, but he can't discern it just yet.

The truth is you don't really think about folks living here. You just think it was always a museum, almost even a replica of some other real thing. Like the Mayflower II up in Plymouth, Mass. They try to make it just like the one his ancestors came over on, and they dress up in costumes and tell you their pilgrim names, give you all the rah-rah about what they ate and where they slept. It's insulting, really. Did any of those fake pilgrims claim to be a Quimby? No they did not. So you can forget any kind of historical accuracy with the facts of the situation.

Here though, you have America at its finest. You've got entrepreneurs like this guy in the painting with big money and big ideas. You've got the architect with even bigger ideas, about respecting nature but defying it too. As if to say, sure, we Americans believe in gravity, but we won't let it keep us down.

Josiah Quimby finds that his initial idea has completed processing: he's going to hire a painter to make a nice big portrait of himself like this one and give it to Rini.

AMANDA

Arthur's all excited about Mrs. K— again. This time he says she insisted on her own chairs from Venice at the dining table. They are, he says, superior to the famous architect's barrel design because they have three legs and can balance on the uneven flagstone floor. The architect's chairs would have wobbled like vegetable cans on a bumpy surface. Amanda likes that the chair backs look like jigsaw puzzle pieces. She finds the famous architect's style a bit relentless when it comes to straight lines and cool curves and she approves of Mrs. K—'s rustically ornate choice. And she finds Mrs. K—'s husband to be a lot hotter than she would have expected if she would have thought for a minute to expect anything of a rich person who owned a department store. Old and gray, that's what she would have expected. Bearded.

But she doesn't trust him; he reminds her too much of a certain Motherfucker.

Beside the fireplace, on top of an upside-down tree trunk, is a tray with all sorts of liquor, and Amanda would very much like, assuming the meaning of life is not available, a glass of bourbon.

THE DAUGHTER

The daughter gets right up close to the portrait. "How does it feel," she whispers to the man in the painting, "to be dead?"

JANIE

"Iffy," the man says as they survey the living room.

"Iffy what?" Janie says in a low voice without turning toward him. What strikes her now are the books stretched out on long shelves by the desk. Titles in several languages.

"Iffy like who could live here?" he says.

A woman in the group turns and looks at Janie and the man. Janie smiles reluctantly and apologetically, but the man presses on.

"Seriously, would you want to live here?" he says. At least his voice is low. "It's like a cave."

But Janie has already envisioned herself stretched out on the cantilevered couch with any one of the books in her hands. The tour guide has said something about the family's long-haired Dachshunds, and now a dog has leapt to her lap; a gin and tonic sweats on a nearby tree stump. A swath of light splashes across her legs. She is reading an illustrated copy of *Don Quixote*. At her feet is a volume of—is that a book of Asian art? Yes, and a nearby copy of *The Sorrows of Young Werther*.

"But the fireplace is nice," he concedes. "Nice and big."

Janie studies her fellow tourists. Do they feel what she feels, like they are in the very brain of the architect? Even the young girl seems impressed. Is the man the only one who doesn't get it?

This is what greatness feels like. This is what it feels like when she enters a book and the words erect themselves like a room around her. Why couldn't she have been great? Or married greatness? The man is satisfied by the mundane, the mediocre, the obvious.

"Cool." he says, nudging his elbow against hers, as the tour guide points out the swinging wine kettle that rotates in and out of the fireplace. But does he say anything about the boulder that spills into the living room from the hearth, uncontained?

Now the waddling tour guide directs them up a staircase and through a hallway. He waits until they all pass, and Janie can tell he's counting to himself, making sure none of his little ducklings have wandered down another corridor. This, she senses, is as close as he will come to having children. What is it like? Not to have children.

"I feel like a spelunker," the man says as they climb the rough stone steps, and he grabs both of her hips like an arcade steering wheel.

Two

LILLIAN

Lillian is twelve, almost a decade away from becoming *Liliane*. It is a summer afternoon in the new twentieth century, too hot for play, and she seeks the respite of indoor shade, of her father's dark library. Even the darkness is moist with heat; the dry books seem to sweat. Lillian runs her fingertips over the German words and names, stirs a light dust, studies the residue on her skin. This is the day she discovers Goethe. Her father sometimes recites a verse or reads aloud from *Werther*, but today, Lillian removes a volume and reads for herself. She is drawn, in this heat, to water, to bodiless spirit:

Gesang der Geister über den Wassern

Des Menschen Seele
Gleicht dem Wasser:
Vom Himmel kommt es,
Zum Himmel steigt es,

Und wieder nieder
Zur Erde muß es,
Ewig wechselnd.

Strömt von der hohen,
Steilen Felswand
Der reine Strahl,
Dann stäubt er lieblich
In Wolkenwellen
Zum glatten Fels,
Und leicht empfangen
Wallt er verschleiernd,
Leisrauschend
Zur Tiefe nieder.

Ragen Klippen
Dem Sturz entgegen,
Schäumt er unmutig
Stufenweise
Zum Abgrund.

Im flachen Bette
Schleicht er das Wiesental hin,
Und in dem glatten See
Weiden ihr Antlitz
Alle Gestirne.

Wind ist der Welle
Lieblicher Buhler;
Wind mischt vom Grund aus
Schäumende Wogen.

Seele des Menschen,
Wie gleichst du dem Wasser!
Schicksal des Menschen,
Wie gleichst du dem Wind!

She takes a seat at her father's desk, removes paper from a drawer, inks the pen's nib, and, in her practiced script, translates into English:

Song of the Spirits over the Waters

The soul of man
Is like the water:
It comes from heaven,
It returns to heaven,
And down again
To earth must go,
Ever changing.

When from the high,
Sheer wall of rock

The pure stream gushes,
It sprays its lovely vapor
In billowing clouds
Towards the smooth rock,
And lightly received,
It goes enshrouded,
Softly hissing
Down to the deep.

Cliffs tower,
Opposing its fall.
Annoyed, it foams
Step by step
Into the abyss.

In a flat bed
It slinks down the grassy vale,
And in the waveless lake
All the stars
Feast on their likeness.

Wind is the wave's
Handsome suitor;
Wind stirs up from the depths
Foaming waves.

Soul of man,
How you resemble the water!
Fate of man,
How you resemble the wind!

She holds up the paper and studies the script. She memorizes it in German, then again in English. *Wind ist der Welle / Lieblicher Buhler. Wind is the wave's / handsome suitor.* Pacing the room, she hears voices outdoors and goes to the window. Out on the street is her older cousin Edgar with his chums. They are tossing a ball back and forth, taunting one another. Edgar's armpits show shadows of sweat when he reaches for the ball. Lillian keeps her body behind the heavy drape and watches. In a few months he will leave for Yale, then Europe. Last week he caught her in his arms for a short polka while Uncle played the accordion. She'd clutched his biceps for balance as he twirled her. Perhaps she will write a poem about that. As she watches him from the window, she does not realize that she is speaking aloud, in the low chant of Temple: *Wind stirs up from the depths / Foaming waves.*

FLLW

And POETRY? Why, the poetry in anything is only the song at the heart of it—and in the nature of it.

Gather together the harmonies that inhere in the nature of something or anything whatsoever, and project those inner harmonies into some tangible "objective" or outward form of human use or understanding, and you will have Poetry.

You will have something of the song that aches in the heart of all of us for release.

EDGAR REMEMBERS

I remember when I first met her—and I felt shy and distant before her, for she seemed herself to be remote, to resent intrusion, and I was rather frightened by her beauty—by the startling blueness of her eyes and the lithe, graceful flow of her body when she moved.

And then I remember, cherished memory, when I first knew her—when I sat on the step ladder by the Christmas tree and she handed up ornaments and we talked and suddenly between us there was warmth and closeness—suddenly her eyes were not just blueness, but eyes to be smiled into; the long, lovely fingers were there to be clasped; and remoteness was not a barrier but a shield, and intrusion was not resented, rather nearness desired.

LILIANE

"What about something in this style?" Liliane says. She and the painter are standing side-by-side before a portrait of a nude woman in repose.

It is 1932. She is in the painter's studio, the windows are open to the hot rush of Florence air, and she decides in some combination of this very moment and all the moments that have led her to this one that in her portrait she shall not be clothed. Draped, yes: by fabric caressing her lap, veiling her hair as if she were a young bride, one who might capture her husband's eye yet. But not clothed.

Liliane feels that her teeth have grown to the size of dominoes and knows not how she says, "A gift. For my husband."

But then she knows: it's the German. She could never speak of these things in English. Although they are in Florence, the painter is from Vienna; although Liliane is from America, she is from a family of German Jews. She speaks to the painter in her other tongue, the one that, growing up, she heard rather than spoke: the language of adults. She hides behind the language of a land she never lived in.

But she cannot hide behind a bride's blush: she is more than forty years old.

At last she glances over at the painter—he is trained in the human form, has painted this very portrait; does he blush too?—and capitulates: "We shall add shutters on either side to fold the painting closed, for privacy."

The painter nods, understanding.

What does the painter understand? The painter is Victor Hammer. He is more interested in the forms of letters than of humans; would rather carve images in wood than paint them. But he has a business to run. Despite last year's innovative uncial, his *Stamperia* will not run on sales of his Milton book alone. Hammer obliges his American patroness, who has treated— and funded—him well. Nor does she harbor unrealistic notions about her son, who has come to Florence to study with the painter, and whose eyes, when it comes to art, are superior to his hands. The painter is a printer who understands how to accommodate the wealthy.

Three years ago, in London, Liliane met the painter and commissioned a portrait of her husband. Her husband, of modest size in real life, dominates most of the space on the large canvas with his broad shoulders, and his bent arm extends out from his torso to claim the remaining space. His hand perches like a talon on the scrolled wooden ear of a chair she'd purchased on a previous trip abroad. His other arm crosses over his chest, and that hand clutches the head of a hiking stick to his heart. She purchased the mahogany stick for him too. Yes, that is what one noticed about the portrait, what she planned so precisely: the way he clutched the solid wooden objects that had come from her. Then one noticed the bright red of his sweater vest over the unbuttoned, untucked sport shirt. The deep gaze of dark eyes; the small shadow at the exposed intersection of clavicles. Her handsome husband.

It had been her gift to him, but she had come to think of the portrait as hers. There was the man and there was the portrait, and she could only claim one of the two.

And now she is here to visit Junior, their aimless son, the painter's apprentice, who refuses to involve himself in the family business—the family's very *raison d'etre*. For the family name, which can be traced back hundreds of years in Germany, means "merchant." Their ancestors were merchants of horses and cows, and now the family name is one of the most famous in Pittsburgh. Fittingly, the family of merchants created a department store, named it after themselves, and are now defined by it: *the most beautiful department store in America*. How has she—how have they—raised a son who scoffs at destiny?

Liliane didn't just marry into this name. Theirs was a shared lineage; she was as much a merchant as her husband. First cousins, they'd had to cross the state line to New York to make their union legal. She was quoted in the papers disavowing any romantic aspects of their marriage. But whose business was it anyway? The purpose of their marriage — its *raison d'etre* — was the takeover of the store. Apart, their shares were worth nearly nothing; together, the kingdom could be theirs. She was then but twenty, Junior's age; her cousin, twenty-five.

After the wedding there was the matter of an heir. It was obvious that her new husband knew things about women that one can only learn from women; things that only women who have been with other men know about themselves. And he taught those things to Liliane. Not intentionally, no matter how much she wished it. Liliane knew that for as much as she studied and learned from him, his goal had not been to instruct. His goal, as his fingertips touched the skin of her small breasts or the tense flesh of her thigh, was the pleasure of the moment, the expansion of the empire.

When he'd gotten that from her — Junior was born within fifteen months of their marriage — he struck out to explore and annex neighboring territories. Or was it simply to connect with the local villagers? Sometimes her metaphors got confused.

But those were the years of the Chestnut Blight, the Great War, the Spanish Flu. Everything felt like a damn metaphor.

LETTER FROM EDGAR

Lillian my only love: —

Am wondering as I write if you are smiling as you read especially when I call you my only love? You are and always will be, Lillian, but I do not deserve you, not because I do not want to do what is right, but because of my nature. Do you sometimes love me, Lillian? Please write me as of old, your letters so cold and different, do you feel that way? Answer this, it is very important for me to know.

What a rotter I have been and hope God will make me suffer for it. No doubt he will.

How I wish we were together. Do you? Good night for today. I do even if you doubt it and I am trying really hard to do as you would like me to, but help me. Do not let me drift, it is bad for me. Kiss the boy for me and for yourself like the last one you gave me, I think you meant that one.

Edgar

LILIANE

The worst part about it was that he loved her. The more he loved her, the more it terrified her because he was incapable of loving only her. Because she could not possibly love him more than she did—than she always had—she embarked on what would become a lifelong effort to love him less. Sometimes he made it easy, when his eyes and hands would stray. But sometimes he made it so hard. She never felt closer to him than when he was away for military training, writing letters and wiring her daily from Kentucky and Washington, D.C. *My own dear love*, he wrote. *My love child. Dearest of all and my beloved. Lillian my only love.*

In her weakest, most hopeful moments, she would let herself think that maybe she *could* be his only love. She would find herself at her desk composing, not a letter, but a poem. She would not send it to him. *Do you find it funny*, she would write instead, *to hear that I am writing poetry?* And he would assure her: *No, not funny you are writing poetry. Keep it up, it always was your hobby only you allowed it to die for a time. Send them to me if you will, not that I am a critic, but they are yours and that is something.* She would write back, claiming that the days without him seemed like years. And he would reply: *How the days and weeks fly here. With you, you write, they seem like years. Well in a few more of my weeks and your years, I hope to be allowed a few days with you.*

But when they finally had even a day together, all the love and the poetry would get mixed up again with the heartache and the latest rumor.

Afterward, he would write: *Your few hours with me, did you really enjoy them? I was so hungry for you, not physically so much as just your presence and talk and discussion. After all I need you for all of these and the time will and shall come when it will all be forgotten as well as forgiven. So please be happy. You owe and deserve it to yourself, and besides you promised me you would. Can see you trying to smile now. Not only try but do, and day in and out.*

Yes, if only she would smile: *Keep well and be happy and smile, for when I come back, never anything in your face but a smile, so practice now for me, my love.*

Over and over he would implore: *Smile and be happy, you know we both need it. Especially you, so start at once. Believe me when I say I love you more much more than any woman in the world.*

At home, reading these words by firelight, she would almost smile.

He would close with love for her and Junior: *Give Jr. my love and tell him the days are near when I will see him again and you too my love. Write often and all the news.*

And: *Enjoyed Jr's. note. Tell him I love him more every day as I do you too, dear Lillian. Believe me I need you and am sure you need me.*

And: *Love love and love to you my dear wife.*

And: *Love the kind you long for.*

But: Then it would happen again.

LETTER FROM EDGAR

My love: —

Needless to say a happy New Year to you both and my soul hope is that in 1919 I can show you I am yours and all yours and that life for us in the future will be happy, so much so that the past will be forgotten.

Believe me your husband and love,

Edgar

LILIANE

But he was never *hers and all hers*. Not before 1919, not in 1919, and not since.

She did eventually send him a poem. She was so much braver by post.

And he so much kinder: *How I wish I could write poems in return for the one you sent me. I loved it and my heart melted and I had a little cry all to myself for you. I shall always keep it. It will mean so much.*

She'd included a hint of something in the poem, a desire that she hid behind a metaphor of spring and new life. Encouraged by his response and emboldened by fears caused by his reports on the flu—1,800 out of 10,000 men at camp had already contracted it—she broached the subject directly: what did he think about more children? She painted a picture for him of brothers and sisters for Junior, of family trips to Canada full of camping and fishing. The more she wrote, the clearer the picture became.

Certainly I smiled when I read your view of my future children. "Think it over" you wrote.

But her vision of his future children did not come to pass.

Instead, a decade later she suffered the birth of his daughter by one of their department store's models. He'd named the girl Betty after his own beloved mother and paraded the infant around the store as if she were a legitimate princess.

Liliane found herself happy, nearly, when he left the girl's mother for someone else.

Now in the painter's studio, she removes her robe and sits on the cloth-covered chair before a vanity. She places a gilt jewelry box on an adjacent table. She opens the box and withdraws a purple pearled necklace, which she unclasps and hangs in a single strand over the side of the open case. She lifts her arms so that they are the inverse of her husband's arms in his portrait— his arms stake a claim; hers open to the heavens—and so that she might feel the warm Florentine air brush her skin. She has left a white veil over her head, a thin wall to protect her from the painter's eye, and to thrust her into another time, another context. She is an angel, a bride, a Jewish Madonna. Then she changes her mind, lifts the veil, and holds its sheer edge in one raised hand. "Paint," she says.

The printer paints. *Vanitas*, he will call it. One cannot simultaneously gratify the desperate desires of the moment and create a legacy that lasts beyond the grave. The wealthy are always caught in such a struggle between the future and right now. They forget the spirit. That is what he will capture in this painting. The jewelry, the wealth, and the possessions will be as meaningless after death as beauty is once the bloom of youth has wilted.

Nonetheless there is something about this woman, something behind the furs and pearls—behind the veil—something to do with spirit. Yes, it is as she lifts the veil that he can see that she wants to reveal herself plainly. (So uncharacteristic of the rich, who, in his experience, prefer deception: *le trompe l'oeil*.) Her body, her face, her eyes—he must capture the eyes, the hollow eyes—her very soul laid bare.

EDGAR REMEMBERS

And I remember slowly growing to know her better, knowing her beyond the legends which had been told me in so many versions by so many people, know her for herself. Slowly understanding the intensity of her feelings, the curious pattern of her life, the heights and the depths, the capacity to love and to be loved, the ache in her heart.

LILIANE

Liliane returns to the studio the next day and unties her robe, but before she removes it, she walks to large windows overlooking the street where she purchased her props. Her husband fancies himself a de Medici; the painter, she supposes, a Michelangelo. Liliane, however, feels like one of Michelangelo's *Prigioni*, half formed in the stone of her merchant family. She sometimes wonders how it all might have been different had she married out of her family and taken someone else's name. After yesterday's sitting she gazed at the *Prigioni* in person and thought maybe she could have broken free of the prison. But there, before the half-carved, tortured souls, she'd also understood that even if the *Prigioni* had broken free, they'd still be made of stone. There was no escaping what one came from.

The swish of her open robe creates a flutter of air that touches her like a hundred feathers, and she is reminded of her flesh, of her husband. *Love the kind you long for.* She draws the curtains closed, save one, and surveys the slab of light, the dancing dust. When she returns to her seat and steps out of the robe, she says to the painter *"Chiaroscuro."*

Three

AMANDA

In the group there is a tribe of four very tall Vikings speaking in a Viking tongue and wearing strange leather shoes that would seem to belong to elves rather than Vikings. Two of the Vikings are men and Amanda guesses they are brothers. One large-hipped, large-pored woman must be the mother; a younger woman in a draping dress attaches herself to the blonder of the brothers. She is like a walking window treatment with Bambi eyes and a supermodel pout. The men's sleek-framed glasses seem like they were designed by the famous architect to match the über-mod House. But, Amanda thinks as they crowd into what Arthur says is Mrs. K—'s bedroom, the men don't quite fit in the House, with its low ceilings and closed-in hallways.

Arthur observes the Vikings' lowered heads and notes that the famous architect had a name for tall people: Weeds.

JOSIAH QUIMBY

Josiah Quimby damn near slaps his thigh on that one. Just when you think old Arthur doesn't know a joke from a cantilever, he lets fly on the Norsemen. Weeds! Oh, Rini—

A moment later Josiah Quimby does in fact have a hand on each thigh and is doubled over and panting as mightily as if he had just completed a hundred yard dash.

JANIE

The man laughs at the weeds joke and asks the bent over Harley guy if he's okay. He calls the Harley guy "dude." All the Harley guy can say is, "Oh god oh god oh god" or "I got I got I got." Janie hopes that the Harley guy does not die. But maybe he would like to die here at the famous House. It would be better than dying in oblivion, which is where he no doubt came from. Dying here would be kind of like dying at Disney World. And if he died here now, it would make the news and Janie could say that she was there when the Harley guy died at the famous House. This would raise her level of importance in some people's eyes. Instead of thinking, "She's the one who can't have a baby," they would think, "She's the one who was there when the Harley guy keeled over at the famous House."

Meanwhile the man has placed his hand on the Harley guy's leather back. Janie realizes that what has been bothering her about the Harley guy is that he is wearing a full leather jacket in July. The man's hand is right on one of the wings or flames or whatever they are on the jacket. "Are you sure, dude?" the man is saying. The man is not one to say dude. He is more likely to say "sport," as if he were in a Fitzgerald novel, which Janie has been reading in her pursuit of the classical education she did not receive. He is only saying dude because the guy is a Harley guy. The Harley guy is not responding, and this time she really believes and not just imagines that he will die.

Die, she hears herself thinking. Then it becomes a chant, like a fraternity's *chug, chug, chug*. She thinks: *die, die, die, die —*

THE DAUGHTER

Whoa. She's feeling the ghost vibes superstrong right now. Probably because they're all crowded in and this room is smaller than downstairs where it was three or four rooms in one. But maybe it's also because someone in their group is la ghost. Not one of the men, even though this man with the ponytail who's bent over like a linebacker about to pass out at the line of scrimmage might be a ghost in a few. It's definitely one of the women. There's the wispy woman with the Jolly Green Germans who might get blown off the next balcony like a leaf. Or the loco looking woman whose husband is tending to Mr. Ponytail. But more likely it is the woman who came by herself. She looks normal enough, kind of like Aunt Mimi, actually. But who comes here alone? A ghost, that's who.

AMANDA

What if she is here today to see a man die? What if they are all here today for that reason? Or worse, what if they were here to see the House when a man just happens to die? People can die, just like that, like Dad did. Does that become the reason they are here? Death? Will they all become pen pals, brought together by tragedy? She's never talked to a Viking before.

Amanda wants to kneel on the stone floor, put her face under the motorcycle man's, and ask what he sees, what he feels, what he knows in this very moment that he never knew before. God, he better know something.

She glances at Arthur. Why doesn't he do something other than rub his hands together and look panicked? At least there's a bed. They could help the guy lie down. Surely they can make an exception to the rule about not touching the furniture. But there must be a rule about not dying in the famous House.

Why don't the Vikings do something? If she were a Viking she'd save the motorcycle man, and while she was at it, menace the Motherfucker. Pillage his puny little fiefdom.

But what if, in the end, there was never any reason to be here—as in planet Earth—to begin with? No reason for anything. *You can call it*, she thinks, *another lonely day.*

JOSIAH QUIMBY

But Josiah Quimby is not in the least bit dead or dying. He is in the euphoric thrall of the bliss that follows the terror of determining beyond the shadow of a single man's doubt that he is going to be married to one Miss Rini Novak before summer's end. He damn near calls out a *yee-haw*, but, supposing it would be against Arthur's house rules, he rights himself, takes in a huff of the carbon dioxide he's hyperventilated, and gives his new friend a hog of a hug.

He suddenly has no idea how he has made it this far in life on his own. Oh moments ago he had a virtual heart attack when his treasured and indeed cultivated image of himself as an "Easy Rider" who was "Born To Be Wild" was, contrary to all lyrical sense, going to diiieeee. The only thing that had previously tempted Josiah Quimby to couple was the prospect of propagating a proper heir to the Quimby name, one who was, unlike the boys of Josiah's brother Reb, worthy of the name. (No offense to the boys; it was Reb's fault, and the fault of Reb's Wiccan wife.) But he'd stood his moral and patriotic ground: better to be free. It's what his ancestors came to be. It's what America was all about.

And that's exactly what he would be with Rini, free, a frigging free bird. Something about the tour guide's weeds comment and he knew. Rini told him straight up what he was (short) and wasn't (tall), and she still kissed him like he was going out to do interplanetary battle and might never make it back. That's what you call free.

But it occurs to Josiah Quimby upon the completion of his embrace that the small room is silent, that approximately twenty-two eyeballs are facing his direction, and he needs to provide an explanatory update on his unconditional condition.

"This, my friend," he claps his new friend on the back and looks out to the group, "is among my final days as a single man. And I cannot complain. I cannot."

THE DAUGHTER

A checkerboard…a crossword puzzle…a racing flag…she feels dizz, dizz, what's the Spanish word for dizz—

JANIE

Die, die, die. The word puffs through Janie's mind like a nasty locomotive, and she looks around the room to see if anyone else hears it. But everyone seems focused on the dude who did not die. Even the man, who usually knows when she's thinking if not exactly what she's thinking, is busy congratulating the not dead dude.

AMANDA

So, okay, relief, right? He didn't die! He's getting married! They did not all come here today to witness the death of a motorcycle man, to be bonded by tragedy, to face death vicariously and therefore to better understand their own lives or their fathers' deaths. Definitely relief. No sense in feeling cheated. No sense in warning him about the dangers of love. No sense in feeling claustrophobic, sardined in Mrs. K—'s bedroom with oversized Vikings. The glass doors to the terrace are open. *You can go your own way.* Maybe she'll just step onto the balcony while Arthur, who is visibly relieved and ready to get right back to business, resumes talk about the Picasso print and the Tiffany lamp and the stone fireplace and the matching bedside lamps designed by the famous architect and the special button built in to the built-in nightstand to call the live-in servants and *oof!*—

JANIE

Janie stands with her arms akimbo and the man threads his arm through hers and clasps his hand on her waist. "How about that?" he whispers in her ear, still obviously thinking of the Harley guy, as the tour guide resumes his prattle. "Dude," she whispers back. Or perhaps she says, "Dead." Or, "Died."

So this is the room of the wife? She had her own room? Did not have to sleep with a man every night?

"It's like a hotel room in here," the man whispers.

The man's cell phone is attached to his belt and begins to vibrate against Janie's side. He pulls his arm from Janie's waist and removes the phone even though they were told to turn off cell phones. The tour guide is talking about the large statue of the Virgin Mary nestled into the stone recess of the fireplace and overlooking the bed. Why did Janie think the family was Jewish? How did the Virgin feel about having a baby? What's wrong with the girl?

AMANDA

As Amanda steps over the threshold to the balcony, she is toppled over by something or someone against her back and finds herself flat on the ground, face to face with an ant making its way along a slab of flagstone shaped like the state of Ohio. The ant appears to be heading from Cincinnati to Columbus, just as she did, alone, en route to Pennsylvania. Had she made plans? She was sure she'd made plans, but the plans were with David and where was David? Maybe she hadn't made any plans at all? The only way she could find out, she'd decided, was to get in the car and go to the place where she thought she'd planned to go. If she arrived, spoke her name, and presented her credit card, and they said, "I'm sorry," then she would know she had not in fact planned anything, which would introduce a whole new set of problems.

So on Thursday she followed the itinerary that she'd printed out the day before. In the slot at the base of her driver's side door was a folder full of maps that she printed at work, along with a sheet of paper with the words, "Itinerary: Thursday, July 1," centered and bold at the top. But who was to say that it was Thursday? That it was the first day of July? It took an enormous amount of faith to believe in a single day of the week.

And then she'd passed a barn with a Confederate flag painted across an entire side of the roof (right about where the ant is now). Maybe she wasn't even in Ohio but the Deep South, maybe it was the nineteenth rather than the twenty-first century, not Thursday but Monday. There was a series of large green signs that said Columbus. The historical figure? She had to trust that they meant the place, the capitol of Ohio. Another sign was large and spun in a slow circle, flashing phrases like a secret code: ARE YOUR – HOMETOWN SAVINGS – BANK 88F – LOW INTEREST – RATES THURSDAY – JULY 1 – 12:21PM WE. She could not decipher it.

The good news was that the person at the B&B had, in fact, a name that matched Amanda's on her reservation list. Which seemed to prove something. Like that David was a Motherfucker who'd stood her up.

Amanda is not one to curse. Her stance on such words, especially the F-word, is that they should be used judiciously. Another word that should be used sparely is *love*. But she fucked that up, didn't she?

She would get up now, but there is a body or something on top of hers, so she is content to watch the ant. Her muscles are sore from yesterday, and the weight actually feels nice. Splayed across the threshold, she hears rushing water. *You can call it thunder,* David. *Or a lonely day.*

THE DAUGHTER

I knew it. Oh wow oh wow. You're here. Why are you here? What happened to you? Who are you? Are you sad? Are you trapped? Do you have a message? Do you need help getting to the next realm? Do you need my help? Did you pick me? Oh wow wow. I will help you. Can anyone else see you? Can you pick who sees you? Why me? Did you choose to be here? Why here? Why not Hawaii? There are supposed to be rainbows all the time nonstop in Hawaii. I mean this is nice here with the trees and the waterfall for sure. Ooh, did you live here? Were you a servant? A guest? A visitor? Or did you know someone maybe one of the tour guides here? Are you here all the time or do you go to other famous houses? Or wait oh god wow did you die here like right here in this room you did didn't you—

JOSIAH QUIMBY

Josiah Quimby flies like a free bird over the edge of the bed so as to do all things in his own power to assist his fellow group members, two of whom, damsels, are prone in the doorway. In another bound he flies over them as well, landing out on the balcony at the head of the older young lady, who, with body pressed to the ground, lifts her head, rests her chin beside an ant, and assures him she is a-okay. Then he tends to the younger young lady who is lights out on top of the older young lady. "Mel! Melissa!" cry the parents.

It's a risk but Josiah Quimby lifts the younger young lady at the shoulders, pulls her gently toward him, slips his left hand under her bent knees, and carries her to the open space of the balcony, where he discerns in the slow-motion, sensorially-heightened moment, the *whip-poor-will* sound of nearby whip-poor-wills even above the rush of plunging water. He likens it to the sound of Rini's voice calling out over his gruff motor as they traverse a Sunday afternoon.

Next thing Josiah Quimby knows he's got the girl lying on the ground with her head soft in his lap and the parents are already on their knees calling her name again. The four Norsemen of the apocalypse gather around them like a bunch of trees. Ye Olde Tour Guide looks like he might have the heart attack that Josiah Quimby himself did not just have.

The younger young lady is not going to die on Josiah Quimby's watch, but he notes that she does look perfectly beatific, with the trace of a smile on her apparently unconscious face.

AMANDA

So she got to be face to face with the motorcycle man after all. He had put his goatee down to the level of ant and Ohio and looked straight in her eyes to ask if she was a-okay, and she knew in that moment something she'd never known before. What that was she could not say. She could not say because the moment was over and because what she knew in that moment was not a thing that had a word for it. It was an unknown thing that she knew only in that moment and couldn't even be sure at this moment—just a few moments later—what it was or if she'd actually known it. But she had! It was the thing that everyone tries to talk about at parties. It was the thing she tried to ask her dad after it was too late. It was the thing that everyone tries to find at the bottom of the bottle of bourbon, in the nest of an owl, in the violent swirl of river rapids. But it's not there or there and it has no name and it comes and it goes its own way, goes its own way, and it is because it always goes its own way that it is what it is. If it stayed it would be something else, something that could be named and talked about at parties. It is like — but it is not — a ghost.

JANIE

On the expansive terrace, surrounded by the blasting noise of the water, the man pulls Janie aside. While everyone else is focused on the girl, he clutches Janie's arm, leads her to the opposite corner and says, "Janie, look at me. Janie, that was the agency. Look at me. Janie, they said we're approved, we're on the list, we're going—oh god would you look at me?"

The distance from here to the frothy top of the waterfall would not be what one considers far if looked at horizontally from upstream. Or even if looked at vertically from the bottom up. But measured vertically from up here, the distance is probably death itself. Or maybe not. She has heard of someone falling from an airplane and surviving.

The man's fingers are on her chin, gently, firmly pulling her face toward his. He keeps talking and talking.

"Janie, do you hear me? We've been approved."

His face is so close to hers that she feels the dewy puffs of his breath land on the top of her nose like waterfall spray. Then all she can see is his mouth, open, open wider and wider.

"Janie. We got it. We've been approved. They're going to give us a baby."

And he swallows her.

Four

AHI OPIHELE

◇
◇ ◆ ◇
◇

Five hundred million years ago and all was sea. There was no
name, no one to name it. Sediment layered on sediment—
sand that would become sandstone, coral that would become
limestone. Three hundred million years later and movement,
pressure, an unfolding. The rocks broke apart and smoothed
down. Dinosaurs. Fifty million years ago the land pushed
against itself again. The land rose and the waters gathered,
rushed, and fell from rock after rock.

FLLW

Read the grammar of the Earth in a particle of stone! Stone is the frame on which his Earth is modeled, and wherever it crops out—there the architect may sit and learn.

LILIANE

By 1933 the painting is more or less forgotten.

A mad man is rising to power in Germany.

Junior is on his way home to the U.S.

An aging architect of some former renown has no clients or prospects.

And Liliane's husband has embarrassed her further by paying thousands of dollars to a competing department store (it is this fact that makes her feel most betrayed) to lavish jewels on his most recent conquest. Once conquered, however, one falls. This one fell so quickly that Liliane's husband attempted to return the six diamond and platinum bracelets and to reclaim his cash. But the savvy competitor will not return the money, and now Liliane's husband is doing his battles in court, and the *Pittsburgh Gazette* is documenting the trial for the public and the wife to consume. *Love the kind you long for* indeed.

The Depression has taken its toll on the department store's employees and on the B&O train from Pittsburgh, which has reduced trips to Bear Run. Thus the country retreat for company employees is no longer attended by company employees. The family's primitive wooden quarters, a mail-order cottage, hangs precariously over a ridge. Liliane's husband dubbed it, "The Hangover." Oh how he charms.

To walk through the woods near Bear Run is to walk through populations of ghost trees, their dry, fallen chestnuts rotting on the earth floor. Nineteen hundred acres of blight. Each year, fewer thriving green trees, more ghosts. In just two decades they have all become shades. But their wood is strong and good for fences.

"And furniture," her husband decrees. "Slice some stumps for rumps. The rest will be minibars."

Everyone's favorite spot is on the stream's floor where Bear Run falls in a brisk and noisy shower. Liliane's favorite space is just behind the falling water. She likes to press her back and her palms against the wet rock and imagine a room: a bed, a desk, and a shelf full of books behind the wall of water. This is where one should live. *Strömt von der hohen / Steilen Felswand / Der reine Strahl / Dann stäubt er lieblich.* When she walks through the plane of water to join the others, it is like passing through the transparent gauze that separates this world from the next. She finds the group sunning and picnicking on the oversized rock above.

Her husband is a city boy, but Liliane loves the Pennsylvania country—the perfume of Mountain Laurel, the crick and chirp of insects and birds, the nighttime hush of stars caught in the webs of tree branches — and she loves even more the sharp tug of a trout on her hand-tied fly.

Although the railroad has cut back service, the road from Donegal has just been paved, and there is talk of a new highway that will be built from Pittsburgh to Philadelphia. So Liliane's husband transfers the title of the Bear Run property from the department store's Beneficial and Protective Association to Liliane herself.

"Now," she says to her husband, who is, for the moment, not in love with anyone else, "we need a proper country house."

FLLW

Poetry, Poetic, Romantic, Ideal—

The word "poetry" is a dangerous word to use, and for good reason. Carl Sandburg once said to me, "Why do you use the words 'poetry,' 'beauty,' 'truth,' or 'ideal' anymore? Why don't you just get down to tacks and talk about boards and nails and barn doors?"

Good advice. And I think that is what I should do. But I won't, unless I can get an equivalent by doing so. That equivalent is exactly what I cannot get. Those words—romance, poetry, beauty, truth, ideas—are not precious words nor should they be *specious* words. They are elemental human symbols and we must be brought back again to respect for them by using them significantly if we use them at all, or go to jail.

LILIANE

Liliane leaves the building of a country house to her husband. She focuses instead on the floundering eleventh floor of the department store, which she transforms into a women's boutique that she now calls Vendôme. She has always loved the French flair — so romantic, so poetic — and she renames the eleventh floor just as she renamed herself. Why, she decided years ago, should she be Lillian, as her birth document insists, when she could be *Liliane*?

She fills the boutique with items from her European and Mexican travels. Why be the most beautiful department store in Pittsburgh when you can be *the most beautiful department store in America*?

She steps off the elevator wearing a fox-fur-trimmed red wool coat with three-quarter sleeves that fall just over her long black leather gloves. "Oh, Mrs. K," her secretary says, "you look stunning today."

"Thank you, Mary," says Liliane, removing her gloves.

That morning her husband glanced at her coat and said, "Won't it make you sneeze, dear?" Then he returned his attention to the paper, no doubt reading about himself.

LILIANE

Perhaps her husband has hit bottom this time. Perhaps the spectacle of the trial, the prospect of building a weekend retreat at Bear Run, will keep him close.

But she will not lick her wounds. Liliane instead continues to bandage the wounds of others at Montefiore. Every time she enters the hospital for her volunteer work, she is reminded that there are emotional wounds and there are physical wounds. She prefers to surround herself with the kinds of wounds one can see.

Last week, for example, she tended a young girl who would soon be given stitches to close the sliced opening over her eyebrow. And the scar will remain for life, just as Liliane's husband's scar remains on his face from a fake bout of fencing while in Germany. She recalls learning of it through family talk. Their mutual aunt had poked fun, saying that he had completed his requirements in Europe—he had been hurt in a duel!—and could return home now.

Liliane had always sensed—hoped?—her cousin's future would be joined with hers. Her own parents were first cousins; family always came first. Upon hearing her aunt's news, Liliane stole outside to the garden to ponder her cousin's European wound and her painful desire to dress it.

LETTER FROM EDGAR

My own dear love: —

You say you love me and always will, and on the other hand you say I don't love you or at least not in the same way you love me. Well everyone for himself. I have decided it was best for me, my future happiness, etc. to stay married to you. And what about you, if you come to a different decision it is up to you to act upon it. Know we decided long ago never to try and stay together if we found more happiness in another direction. You certainly owe me nothing, you have been a brick to stick as you have and I love you for that in itself. Do you ever long to belong to someone else? If so I will step aside and wait. If after trying you still love me and want to come back not finding that happiness as you supposed, I will always be ready and hope for you until I die.

Edgar

RICHARD

Perhaps one day a gentleman enters the eleventh floor of the department store in search of a gift for his wife or mistress or secretary and sees a woman bent over a table arranging bone china in place settings. She steps back from the table and observes from several angles before she steps forward again to adjust the spacing of the silverware. The gentleman finds that the woman's ankles remind him of a bird's, and he is a great fan of birds. For one, they can fly. He loves the word *flight*. And what has more sex appeal than a feather? The answer is a woman. A woman is the only thing more beautiful than a feather, and this woman setting the table might be the most beautiful of all.

Perhaps the woman turns around and is not the most beautiful, but something else. The most elegant, the most on fire. More than he expected of a shop girl, which gives him some pause, but he is ever up for the latest challenges of the female species. He's had enough with preening cockatiels anyway. What he's got himself here is a hawk. He can tell this without even having talked to her, and he is ready for the commencement of the games. "Excuse me, miss," he says, and spies a very large diamond perched like an egg on her ring finger. "Madame," he corrects himself, delighted.

Perhaps another woman walks up at that moment and asks if she might help him. Suddenly there are two birds, one offering to help him, another who has not said a word. One has youth; the other, it is quite clear, breeding. Fleeting as it is, youth is overrated. Good breeding is like a pearl in an oyster. Good breeding is to be mined like gold. "My question was for the Madame," he says without so much as a glance back at the lovely youth, hoping she hops off like a baby bird who can't fly. The Madame's eyes bounce from his feet to his face with the casual arc of a rubber ball. "Thank you, Ethel," she says, and blinks the youth away. When young Ethel has left, Mother Bird takes a breath. "How," she coos, "may I help you, sir?"

Let the games begin.

LILIANE

Liliane decides to tell him that her name is Ilia. She cuts the heart right out of the middle and gives it to him.

"Ilia?" he says. And then he surprises her: "Like the French— *Il y a.*"

They are in his car. They are parked near the muddy Allegheny like teenagers. Liliane had thought she heard her name echo all over France—*Liliane, Liliane, Liliane*—only to discern that, of course, it was *il y a, il y a, il y a.*

There is this. *There is* that.

How did he know? Who is this man with the sleek Studebaker and out-of-state license plates who knows her French secret? *Il y a un homme. Il y a un voiture.*

She was going to protect herself with the fake name and laugh to herself as he called her the equivalent of *There Is*. "Oh, *There Is*," he would say, "kiss me." And *There Is* would kiss him if she felt like it. And she supposed she would feel like it. Like kissing. This man would do. But this man—he says his name is

Richard—has already penetrated the first wall of her resistance, and most of her other walls are just as flimsy.

"Are those tears?" Richard says. His thumb reaches for the tear on one cheek as his lips taste a tear on the other, and he whispers, "*Il y a des larmes, Ilia?*"

Soon enough Richard drives away, toward the state on the license plate, or somewhere else. After Richard there is Luke, the one with the camera. And the wife.

Then dear Laszlo.

Oh, but it is hard to keep one's dignity when one is aging, naked, and panting.

FLLW

Any house is a far too complicated, clumsy, fussy, mechanical counterfeit of the human body.

LILIANE

Slowly, quickly—time is relative, shifting, fleeting, irrelevant—
the timeless house is designed and built at Bear Run. Liliane is
given the premiere room, the gravity-defying balcony.

AHI OPIHELE

◇
◇ ◆ ◇
◇

And then, one day, people: Monongahela, Lenape, Shawnee, Iroquois. And with them, names. The river that twists and turns: *Yawyawganey*. The site of rushing waters and powerful falls: *ahi opihɔle*. "It turns very white."

Then arrived a young George Washington battling the British, the French, the Indians. Then the Irish, German, and English immigrants; farmers, hunters, and trappers. Then came a Whiskey Rebellion, the return of General Washington.

Then came mills, mines, and timber. Then came Masons, then came Merchants: the Kaufmanns, their weekends, their Mr. Wright.

The name of the nearby town of frothing water: *ahi opihɔle*, Ohiopehelle, Ohiopyle.

Five

JANIE

It is dark, it is dark. She hears his body as if through a stethoscope—the echo of his breath, the rushing liquid of what must be his blood. Now his stomach acid will dissolve her and her plans into nothing.

Recently Janie has decided that she will enroll in some courses at the college where she works. They're free, after all. She used to believe that all the books on the Classics table at the bookstore were supposed to be more or less like exercise or healthy eating: worth it if you could get through them. But she found herself turning pages the way she imagines a marathoner turns laps—with a buzz.

After the last few years of regularly scheduled visits to fertility doctors, the calendar for the rest of Janie's life now looked quite open.

She knows that just as not everyone enjoys running marathons, including herself, not everyone enjoys reading. But she does. Next week she has appointments set up with a person in the English department and another in Education. She's used to so many appointments, and she's just glad she will be able to keep her clothes on for these.

Did she tell the man about these appointments? She did not.

She has no idea how rockets work, but aren't there always two sections? And in the burning heat of take-off, the rocket breaks apart, with one piece heading for Mars or wherever and the other veering off in the opposite direction? She is not sure which section is her and which is the man, but she knows they are in two parts flying or falling in different directions.

She will not miss her appointments.

The man's ribs are the bars of a prison. "Let me out! Let me out!" she calls to the man.

"Janie," he whispers, "open your eyes."

THE DAUGHTER

Let you out of what? Out of the House, out of your body, out of your mind? Which part is which? Like which part needs to be let out and where would it go? I can hold your hand and we can go for a walk. I can take you as far as you want, but we should leave little clues behind so I can get back, like they teach at Girl Scouts. We can cut marks into trees, break branches, turn over rocks. Or, can we? Do things work differently here so we can't scratch a tree? Do you know what purple is? Like purplish-blue? You look really purplish-blue. Or everything around you does and it smells like science class when the teacher opens the jar with the dead pig and one time I almost fainted when he did that because it tingles and bubbles right up the nose and the pig is shriveled and bald and did I tell you you're purplish-blue and how it smells…

AMANDA

Amanda rises and stands just beyond the shadow of the extended eave. She is not quite outside, and yet she is. The sky has the gray-blue haze of summer, with a gauze of clouds stretched thin like a veil. Her group huddles around the girl, and it occurs to Amanda that this large balcony is a framed canvas for God — or Dad. If they were to look down, they would see the young girl looking straight up at them — unless her eyes are closed. Amanda can't tell from here. Around the girl, the circle of others must look, to God or Dad, like flower petals. In the opposite corner of the terrace is the man who was just on his cell phone. He is clutching the upper arms of the woman he came with. To God or Dad it might look like they are dancing, but Amanda can see how tightly he is clutching the woman, and the idea that she can see something God or Dad can't is not something she wants to think about. But God or Dad would see Amanda standing by herself, going her own way, not going anywhere, and in that they would be correct.

IRENE

So, Josiah Quimby. A real gentleman, you know? Seems like it anyway. God knows I've been fooled before, which is why, according to Tammy, I'm such a bitch when I first meet someone. I was only moderately evil to Josiah, what with letting him sit in some silence after the uninvited peck on the cheek and then telling him he was a shorty—not that I can talk, ha! But the next thing I knew he kissed me for real, and damn if I didn't kiss him back. He left me sitting on the bar stool, my thighs feeling like I was straddling that cycle he rumbled off on.

AMANDA

On their third date, David had said, "It's the end of the world as we know it. And I feel fine." "Good for you," Amanda had replied. Then he drove her to the edge of Ohio and led her under a massive yellow bridge that held up eight lanes of highway over the murky Ohio River. "We can walk to Kentucky on the catwalks," he said. Under the bridge? She did not feel fine.

But she followed him as he led her up the gravelly hill to where the bridge touched down, depositing the highway onto the earth of Ohio. She followed him along the steel grate, heading toward Kentucky, clutching the cold bars at her hips. She watched the ground drop away from her as if she were walking up rather than out.

She did not feel fine. And she didn't know if these sorts of adventures were what made her think about this strange and new David as she fell asleep, as she woke up, brushed her teeth, and drove to her job at the pension company. Or if it was because her dad was dead and she needed something else to think about.

A few weeks earlier on their second date he'd driven her to an abandoned barn, grabbed her hand, and led her through a door broken off its rusty hinges. She was sure the owners or their banjo-dueling kin would pull up any moment with a pickup truck and a full gun rack. A homeless person would emerge from under a pile of hay in the corner. A coven of teenage Satanists would pour blood through the gaps in the rafters and then kill and eat them. When these things did not happen, she thought something else still might. The rusted out tractor would suddenly start up and run them over. The silo would drop an avalanche of corn on them.

This was how she believed life worked. You go along your safe little path, day by day at the pension company, avoiding danger, and one day it—danger, death—comes and gets you or your dad anyway.

Some of her clients saved up all their pension money, believing that they would make it to sixty-five, and instead, Amanda would get a call informing her that the client was dead. Which must be why so many other workers called as soon as they finished a short-term construction job and requested to be paid out. "Well, Mr. Johnson," Amanda was trained to say, "I have to inform you that there are several fees for early withdrawal. There is a twenty percent fee for the government, a ten percent fee for processing, a twenty-five dollar penalty fee, and another fifteen percent fee for doubting your future."

In the barn David had held her by the waist as she climbed up a rusty ladder to make sure no one was up in the hayloft. As she lowered herself back down, he slipped his cool hands under her shirt, grabbed her in a bear hug around the waist, and pulled her backward on top of him and hay. David's legs were straddled, with his knees up for support, like he was giving birth to her, and she was breech. Dust from the hay swirled angrily around them. That was the moment (she thought) they stopped being strangers. They lay there for a couple minutes, looking up at the long lines of light coming through the roof, the flat planes of floating dust. David's chest pushing her up, letting her back down.

THE DAUGHTER

I feel like I know you do I know you? Do you know me? Do you follow me around in my life? Can you see me when I'm taking a shower? When I said that about the time I was dissecting a pig well that was in high school but I've never been to high school I'm only twelve but I remember dissecting this dead animal and it makes me want to cry to see you all of a sudden why is that why do I want to cry do you know it's because of you isn't it it's because I know you or knew you and now you're gone except you're here and that's what makes me so happy I'm sad you were there weren't you when I was in high school dissecting that pig they called it a fetal pig because it was a baby and something about that whole little body being shriveled and shiny and that smell you were there and I haven't even been there yet and now you're here do you remember the pig and the scalpels do you remember how we would drive after class to the state park and get lost on the paths in all those acres and acres of woods yes it was just like the woods here acres of them and how we'd stop at the side of the lake and sit on a bench and I'd wonder if you were going to kiss me or if I was going to kiss you and wishing you would or I would and at the same time that you wouldn't because what is more perfect than a private glassy lake and our feet on pine needles and stones and the smell of laurel and pine and the sides of our arms touching as we both look ahead to the future and wanting to kiss and be kissed except kissing is gross so why am I saying all of this to the future the future what future there is no

JOSIAH QUIMBY

But now her smile has flatlined and tears are forming like sap at the meeting of her eyelids. Josiah Quimby would like to cradle the girl in his arms and hold her for a spell, but she is not his to hold. The mother seems to take the tears as a good sign that the girl is not comatose, but Josiah Quimby thinks behind those closed eyes, this girl is rumbling with more power than a motor. Which is why he'd like to hold her steady and quiet instead of shaking her shoulders and yelling into her ears like her folks keep doing.

AMANDA

Yelling is not going to make the girl wake up. Just like inviting David here did not make him come. Or wishing did not make her dad alive.

On the catwalk David had called out, "Yoohoo!" Amanda listened to the tiny echo that answered his call: *you who?* He was far ahead, had already abandoned her. She had been wrong about the moment in the barn. They were still strangers. Instead of progressing from strangers to intimates, as she thought happened in relationships, she and David would remain strangers who, every now and again, would share an intimate moment.

She caught up to him and pressed the side of her face between his shoulder blades, cushioned by his coat. She breathed in the smell of river, soap, and something that reminded her of sex. I feel fine?

"Look," he whispered.

Only after she opened her eyes did she realize she must have closed her eyes, and that he must have waited for her to catch up.

She grabbed his waist with one arm to steady herself and stood on tiptoe to peek over his shoulder in the direction he was facing. Steel beams criss-crossed one another, leaving dark geometric shadows; the loud drone of cars passing overhead filled her ears.

"What?" she said, quiet, but also loud.

She did not feel fine. They were too high from the ground, and there was too much free space to fall. Her dad was dead. She would turn carefully around and return to the car. She would wait for David to take her home for the last time.

"An owl," he said.

All she saw was shadow and steel.

"She's got a nest," David said. "See?" He turned his body toward Amanda's and lowered his face so that they were cheek to cheek. All the while he kept a hand firmly on the railing, and she kept her arm around his jacketed waist. He aligned their vision by pressing his cheek to hers, and he pointed with a free hand. "Over there, under those rafters."

And then she saw it. It was perched in a corner and caught in the shadow of an angle. Its face was flat and round.

She reached into the inside pocket of her jacket and pulled out a flask that she had recently purchased for the novelty of it. Who owns a flask? Who uses one? Old men from the 1800s. So she'd bought it for herself, filled it halfway, then a bit more, with bourbon, and stuck it in her pocket. Now, she decided, was a brilliant time to christen it.

Six

LILIANE

Would the cantilevers fall, would the house collapse? These questions are among the most important to Liliane's husband.

"There's a new crack," he says. "Did you see it?"

Liliane knows the house is sound. There are many things she does not trust in this life, but she trusts the house and its builder. Where her husband enlists experts and second opinions on the house, she would like to enlist experts and second opinions on this life of theirs.

"There are always new cracks," she says, thinking of the rumors that are circulating once again. It was not so much that she heard the rumors as that she walked in on their hushed exchange, the sudden silence, the guilty avoidance of her gaze. The rumors were always the same.

"I've got to get someone to run tests again," he says.

They are on the terrace outside the living room. The sun is just clearing the row of trees, spilling its light onto Liliane's legs. Soon her whole body will be covered in sunlight. She drops a few bits of chicken onto the patio and the dogs gobble it up. Her husband paces, pausing to study the concrete seams on the balcony. Sometimes it is his handsomeness that pains her the most.

"Fallingwater, all right," he says, loud enough to be heard over the rushing water, but apparently to himself. He rests his arms on the parapet, tense, and the weight of his upper body bears down on them. "This house is going to fall right into the goddamn water, Liliane," he says, turning toward her. "Let's just pray it happens on a weekday when we're not here."

LILIANE

It had been a busy week at the store, with delivery problems for not one but two of Vendôme's customers. Liliane had had to appease them with flowers and personal notes of apology. But tonight will be a grand party at Aspinwall. Her husband will play the role of host and escort Liliane into the room, where moving and still cameras will await them. Winter was coming, but she is indoors, so the sleeves of her full-length dress are short, capped, and tied. The back plunges open in a wide V.

Her husband arrives at her door, and when the servant opens it for him, Liliane makes sure to have her exposed back toward him, to be casually fitting an earring on an ear like a scene in a motion picture.

"Hello, Kitty," she hears him say.

"Mr. Kaufmann," Kitty replies. "Mrs. Kaufmann is almost ready."

"That's alright," he says, stepping further into the room. "It's quite a crowd down there. You'll be needed."

Liliane holds her earring, wondering if he might ever look, if he might ever see her and want only her. If she were a showgirl? A store girl?

"Go ahead, Kitty," Liliane calls, and with one last touch of her hair, she rises and turns toward her husband, who is in fact looking at her. He looks pleased.

"Hello," he says.

"Hello there." She feels like a girl of twelve again, blushing at her older cousin.

When she joins him at the door's threshold, he touches his fingertips to her bare back, and with a delicate pressure says, "Don't forget to stand up straight, dear."

For sometimes she slouched a bit.

LILIANE

The exotic artist rests her crippled legs on the couch at Bear Run. Liliane's husband helped the raven beauty elevate her legs and arrange her long skirt, and now Liliane must watch him watch her. He and the young gallery owner hover over the poor woman like all the birds and monkeys she paints around her head in self-portraits.

Earlier that evening—it was hard to believe it had been the same evening, a state away and train ride hence—Liliane and her husband attended an exhibition of the artist's paintings in New York, and when it came time to decide on a purchase, it was Liliane who made the choice.

While her husband was occupied with praising the beautiful artist's rich colors, and tantalizing her with descriptions of the house at Bear Run—"That's right," he'd proclaimed, "*Time* magazine!"—Liliane gazed at one painting after another. Liliane knew something of the dark artist's own famous, philandering husband, so even as the artist batted her long eyelashes like Oriental fans at Liliane's husband, Liliane could not hate her.

Liliane was not interested in the paintings with monkeys and birds. Instead she was drawn to the one of the artist with an open gash in her upper thigh. One hand holds back a white skirt, exposing the bleeding wound. The other hand hides behind the fabric folds, between the spread legs. Plant roots cover the subject-artist's face like a veiny veil. Behind her flies a banner with the words: *Recuerdo de la herida abierta*.

Remembrance of the open wound.

Liliane, familiar with open wounds, had turned to her husband, the artist, and the curator. She could see what the men could not, or cared not to see: that the now smiling painter was, in the painting, simultaneously bleeding and masturbating.

"We will take this one," Liliane had said.

FLLW

Each material has its own message and, to the creative artist, its own song. Listening, he may learn to make two sing together.

LILIANE

They have rich but not famous guests over today. Three other couples who, following the excitement of the house tour, have settled into uninspired conversation in various parts of the living room. The doors and windows are open and a small breeze comes in and out. Liliane's husband is smoking a cigarette. She removes it from his hand, walks out to the balcony, leans against the ledge with the top half of her body extended out over the water like she might fly, and smokes the cigarette herself. There has been little rain in recent weeks, and Bear Run's water falls thin. When the water is low like this, her husband calls it Bear Crawl.

"Let's take a dip," she suggests to the floundering crew.

Within thirty minutes, the group is ankle deep in the always-cold waters, and not a one of them is wearing a stitch of clothing. The men's parts shrink and expand, and Liliane's husband catches her stealing glances at the uncircumcised among them. He laughs at her, and she splashes him in return.

The cook watches from the kitchen window.

FLLW

Look about you at earthly forms! Trees, flowers, the reactions to one another of the elements in sky, earth, and sea.

LILIANE

"What is that?" Liliane's husband asks.

It is January 1940 and has been more than a year since the art show in New York. The painting arrived safely but has not been hung until now. Outside, a soft snow falls and melts; inside, a freshly-stoked fire blazes in the hearth. The entire house smells of smoking wood.

"What is what?" she says.

"That." He is seated at the table, and before him is a plate of scrambled eggs, a glass of orange juice, a mug of coffee. He is pointing straight ahead at the stone wall.

"It's a painting."

"I know that."

"Perhaps you remember the artist," Liliane says. "Quite lovely. We had her here the night we purchased the painting." *You hung all over her like a monkey. You tried to bed her in this house.* "It's one of her many self-portraits."

"Jesus, Liliane, I know all that! What's the painting doing here? And where'd the other one go?"

"What's funny," Liliane says, "is that the Mexican painter is part German, like us. Could you tell?"

The famous Mexican painter had confessed to Liliane the next morning, after having sex with either Liliane's husband or with the curator (all Liliane knew was that the woman had sex with someone — it was not until Liliane's husband arose, despondent, that she discerned he had lost to the curator), that the painter's own mother was also a Kaufmann from Germany. So the lovely painter's family, which might have been Liliane's family, had also been merchants, and now the painter was a Mexican Communist. Liliane hoped she might be related to the painter, but they could, in the end, find no direct links. So the matter was unresolved, and Liliane found herself feeling like her own defeated husband must have felt when he tried to invite himself into the guest room the night before.

Now her husband responds by telling her to move the painting and to return the other one, a drab landscape. But Liliane thinks the stone partition opposite the fireplace, prime real estate that opens to the living room where she knows he conducts his dalliances, is the perfect place for this piece.

Liliane had also purchased another painting from the Mexican German woman: *Mi Nacimiento*, My Birth. Her husband should be glad that she hasn't placed *it* on this wall. It is a small painting with a woman, naked and dead, on a bed. A sheet covers the woman's face and torso and head, and coming forth from her open legs is the half-conscious head of the painter. Above the bed, a daggered Virgin of Sorrows looks on. On the scroll painted across the bottom there are no words.

When Liliane gave birth to Junior she feared she was dying. She thought, as her entire being flared in pain, that this would kill her. But there had been a painting of the Virgin Mary on the wall of the Catholic hospital, and the image watched over her. The Virgin remained placid, unworried, and Liliane came to understand she would not die—not here, anyway. This was birth, not death. *Mein gott*, were they so similar?

And somewhere between birth and death was sex. She had once thought sex would kill her. Later she would think not having sex would kill her. His sex with others would kill her. And so she found Richard, Luke, Laszlo. And now they were gone. It would all, over the next dozen years, kill her. Stoops, Stoops.

Seven

AMANDA

Later that night, after the bridge and the owl, Amanda lay in her bed with bourbon in her blood, pulsing to the beat of high school marching band drums. Her apartment window was open, and she could hear the band practicing, and the truth was, she didn't know they were drums for about twenty minutes. Her anxiety had grown as her heart seemed to pump at so many different tempos, and no sooner did she think, "I'm going to die, just like Dad," than she realized the beating was not inside her at all, but elsewhere.

"And isn't that life," she said aloud.

"Hoo hoooo oo oo," replied a bird, which she took to be the mourning dove she always saw perched in her empty planter, and which she took to mean, "Yes, that's life."

"What do *you* know?" she called.

Had the dove gotten itself drunk fifty feet above the land only to stagger farther out the catwalk until it was a hundred or more like three hundred feet above the freaking river?

And had it, having seen an owl and having hovered drunkenly over the brown current, clutched the cold steel rail with one hand and unbuttoned the pants of its date with the other? She didn't suppose so. Not without opposable thumbs.

And did the dove let go of the rail to take another hot drink and then practically bite the ear off its date as the highway traffic rumbled above? That would require a dove's date to have ears now, wouldn't it?

And did the dove say to her date, as she clutched two cold steel rails and let the date pull her pants down and thrust in and against her, *I love you*?

And did the dove, in the empty silence that followed, repeat herself?

JANIE

Janie works at one of the regional campuses of the big state university doing who knows what. She was hired to work in the bursar's office, but she never met any actual bursar. She would answer the phone and say, "Bursar's Office," but no one ever asked to speak to the bursar, and she never transferred any calls to a bursar. At least if one works in the chancellor's office, one occasionally gets a glimpse of the chancellor. Janie began to sense she was working for and referring to something that did not exist, and this unnerved her. That no one else seemed to notice or care unnerved her more. So she asked to be moved to Academic Affairs, where she imagined all sorts of scandalous activities took place. But when she got there, she found neither academics nor affairs, just a bunch more phones and files and unseasonable, unmatching outfits on her coworkers. Janie got cold from the summer air conditioning and hot from the winter overheating too, but that was no excuse for not putting certain clothes in a cedar chest for six months of the year. How could people put on such clothing combinations and walk out of the house?

Janie didn't know what an Associate was, but all of the administrative offices had been temporarily relocated to the Associates Building while the Administration Building underwent renovations for the first time since the university purchased it from a finance company that no longer existed. Janie already missed the former interior with the worn-out plush feel of middle-aged men smoking through board meetings before returning to their tragic lives. The new interior would surely look just like every other Exciting New Renovation on campus, with smooth light wood, crescent shaped desks, modular lighting, and lightweight chairs on wheels. It was, Janie believed, the equivalent of replacing Willy Loman with Harry Potter, which was exactly what they were doing in the English Department. Janie read every word of every literature course description over the last several years, planning to take advantage of her tuition discount, and the changes were as depressing as those made to the buildings. She wanted to get an English degree before all the courses were about graphic novels and vampires.

In the Associates Building, where they waited out the remodeling, there were no windows, and the jaundiced lighting caused coworkers to ask one another if they were feeling sick. "No, I'm fine. Are you sick?" "No." "Oh." "Well."

All of the offices and departments that had been in separate hallways of the Administration Building were now jigsawed into one vast room on the second floor of the Associates Building. Hundreds of cubicles were splayed throughout the low-ceilinged, dim-lit room. One coworker battled the gloom with holiday decorations. Last week her cube was lined with small American flags, like a miniature garden fence. There was a red, white, and blue accordion streamer draped between beige metal filing cabinets, and the shelves of an empty metal bookcase were arranged like a dining room hutch, with upright paper plates and cups adorned with fireworks.

Another coworker had an expensive sunlamp on her desk, even through the summer. She communicated in the subjunctive tense. Janie listened to her on the telephone with students: "What would you say if I told you there was a hold on your account?" "What would you say if I asked how soon you would have your bill paid off?" "What would you say if I asked you if you want a baby?"

Janie hunkered down, opened her three-ring binder, and read the *Collected Stories of Franz Kafka* hidden inside. Later, at home, she propped the same book on her recipe stand and read as she made spaghetti and meatballs from memory for the man.

AMANDA

How she wished she could take it back. Not because of the silence. No, even in the moment that followed, when his mute tongue crept into her mouth like a night slug, she didn't want to take it back. It was a gift she had given him, her love — or her proclamation of it — and she expected nothing in return.

But, afterward, when it was not her heart but the high school drums that were beating, she wanted to take her love, or proclamations of it, back, so it would be inside and not outside of her, elsewhere. She didn't mind so much that he hadn't returned the sentiment. What bothered her was that she wasn't even sure he had *accepted* it. If she gave him a twenty dollar bill, she would not expect him to give her anything in return; she would just ask that he close his fist tightly around the bill and put it in his pocket. Better yet, put it in a pension fund and let it grow over time. But she felt like she had given him a twenty-dollar bill, and he had let it go into the air. That it had fallen slowly from the catwalks, catching air currents, until it landed in the river and eventually got caught in a tangle of roots or on a rusty shopping cart.

THE DAUGHTER

love. I remember it all now. How we fell in love three years from now, how we learned how to drive, played basketball in your driveway, kissed at the state park, got poison ivy. How you broke up with me for someone else two years later. Do you have any idea how you hurt me? And how we kept coming back together as friends and first loves in high school and college. How you moved away and I got married. Sometimes we would call and say, "Hey, how's your job? How's your life? How's my first love?" And at Christmas you'd come back to see your family and give me a call and my husband would let me go see my first love for a drink. You never know when you're having your last drink with your first

THE DAUGHTER

love. You never know that you'll come back from work one day, thinking how did I end up with this job, thinking I'm almost thirty it's time to make a change, thinking I've got to get coffee and juice boxes before tomorrow, thinking did I write that check for the preschool, thinking why is there a note on the table with my first love's sister's name and phone number written on it. And then your husband holds your shoulders firmly and explains that your first love is

THE DAUGHTER

dead. Do you understand? Dead. You're dead. You can't talk or eat or kiss because you are—

who are you?

JOSIAH QUIMBY

Josiah Quimby looks a baker's dozen years into the future and hopes his little offspring is like this youngster here. The kind of girl who would carry the Quimby name into the future of America, and not trade it for the name of some boy whose family did not found the U.S. of A. This girl, he can tell, is going to keep her head and her name when it comes to men, and he wonders for the first moment whether, when he offers the Quimby name to Rini, she will accept it—the name, not the man—and whether he might respect her somewhat more if she declines.

Now the girl is sobbing and he wishes it wouldn't be entirely inappropriate to stroke her hair until she stops.

AMANDA

The trip to the famous house had been her idea. It had been months of their strange Morse code of dating—long silence; short, intense encounters; long silence—but those times were the closest she'd come to anything like happiness in the past year since her dad died. For months her grief had felt like the sharp pain and numbness of a full-body saline injection, and suddenly there was David, who took her to places she'd never been in a town where she'd always lived, put his arms around her, and made her feel something else. She had called it love. Twice.

She was at work, reviewing a pension plan—with its concrete calculations and expectable projections for ten, twenty, thirty years into the future—when she thought: yes, a plan. So she planned a weekend of biking and balconies. Hiking and wine. What about whitewater rafting, she'd said. Class 4 rapids? She took his yes to mean yes. She took her planning to mean they had plans.

The plan they agreed on was that she would pick him up at his apartment Thursday morning. But when she arrived at 9:00

a.m., with two fresh Caribou coffees in the cupholders between the front seats of her car, he wasn't there. Knock-knock. Ding-dong. Ring-a-ling. Voicemail. Hey, it's David. Leave me a message. David, it's me. I'm at your place to pick you up for our trip. Where are you? Hey, it's David. Leave me a message. Me again. Train's leaving the station, ha ha. Coffee's getting cold. Call me! Hey, it's David. Leave me a message. I'm starting to get worried. We were supposed to leave almost an hour ago. Hey, it's David. Leave me a message. —— Hey, it's David. Leave me—. Hey, it's David. Hey—. Hey—. Knock-knock. Who's there? Amanda. Amanda who?

THE DAUGHTER

Liliane? That's a pretty name. I'm Melissa. I'm very tired, Liliane. Very tired.

LILIANE

✤

I understand. But do you know: I never had a daughter. My husband had a daughter but I didn't. Another woman had my daughter, and sometimes I would see the girl and her mother when they came to the store. By the time the girl was your age, though, they did not come around, the woman or the daughter. You look like she might have looked. And like I looked at your age when I first read Goethe. Have you read Goethe? His "Song of the Spirits over the Waters"—that is the English translation—is what this house is about, *lieb.* Listen:

> The soul of man
> Is like the water:
> It comes from heaven,
> It returns to heaven,
> And down again
> To earth must go,
> Ever changing.

Can you hear it, *lieb*? The falling water? The soul of man and girl?

When from the high,
Sheer wall of rock
The pure stream gushes,
It sprays its lovely vapor
In billowing clouds
Towards the smooth rock,
And lightly received,
It goes enshrouded,
Softly hissing
Down to the deep.

Do you see? I was destined, even before I discovered the poem, to live here, to die here, where the soul rises and falls like water. Where the pure jet of water streams from the high, steep wall of rock. Your destiny is already in action, my dear. You already long for a future that will hurt. That is what this house is about, *lieb*: the fate of man and girl. Aspire, expire. Aspire, expire. Defy—

No, that is not what I want to say to a young soul, a dear girl. I want to say that I died here. I died before I expired, do you see? I defied and died—

Cliffs tower,
Opposing its fall.
Annoyed, it foams
Step by step
Into the abyss.

No, no. I am sorry. I do not mean to speak of the abyss. I tell you to love. Please, *lieb*. Love and love, despite *la herida*. *La herida abierto* of your first love.

Do you understand Spanish? German? Do you smell the rhododendron? Do you hear the warblers? Have you read Goethe? It is time. *The soul of man resembles the water.* Do you hear the falling water? *The fate of man resembles the waves.* It's just beneath you.

FLLW

The present is the ever moving shadow that divides yesterday from tomorrow.

Eight

LILIANE

And then one day she wakes up in her bed at Bear Run and she has been married for forty years. *They* have been married, of course, but they have been married in such very different ways that she marks it as a personal milestone.

She recalls their train ride to New York, two lifetimes ago now. The trip out of state had felt both illicit, since what they were doing was not even legal in their native state, and urgent. They could scarcely look at each other.

When they got off the train and were met by the reporters from the *Times*, she told them more than they needed to know only because she could not tell her cousin herself. It was to reassure him that she said (and later gasped to see it in print): "There is no romance connected with our marriage, except that we came here in a special train, if you consider that one."

But it had worked. By the time her cousin became her husband he was more relaxed and even awkwardly affectionate as he navigated the various postures involved in posing for photos as a couple. An arm on her shoulder. A hand covering hers. She laughed at his attempts, and he laughed back. It was the first thing they shared as a married couple: the awkwardness of having been cousins first. Their first affections came from trying to act married together.

Even if they had gotten married for the family business, they had, in fact, gotten married. And she knew it was only because she had told the reporter that she understood the marriage was not about romance, that, on the train ride back home, in the deep darkness—which came late in the evening so soon after the solstice—their bodies found romance.

After that it was always in the dark. No names spoken, no words exchanged. He spoke through his hands that held and shifted her, and she replied by bracing and clasping. A mute, anonymous encounter. An encounter she came to crave, but too soon she grew large with Junior. While her body was busy with that, her husband's began its lifelong drift. Perhaps he did not like the namelessness of the dark. He found lunchtime gals. Gals with names like Pauline and Candace.

They had been married during the Chestnut Blight and sometimes Liliane was sure that their marriage had been infected; that the *endothia parasitica* had entered their marriage tree through a crack; that it had spread to the inner portion; that it had caused infection in the leaves, then the limbs, spreading until the whole thing was dead.

It was so many years ago now, the wedding, the blight, but

weren't they still chopping down dead chestnut trees at Bear Run all these years later?

She hears him shuffling about in his adjacent bedroom. Now he pads down the stone hallway in his slippers.

For a moment the night before she had entertained the idea of inviting him to her room, to seduce him with reminders of her large balcony, a common joke about the house. "We can watch the sky turn dark on the longest day of the year," she considered saying. And even now she awakens with a girlish urge to hold his hand and walk barefooted in the waters, to hide from the servants in her favorite space, the recess of the rock behind where water falls like a tongue hanging out of the mouth of the house.

But these fancies have nothing to do with the marriage she actually lives, the one where she will arrive downstairs to find oversized hollyhocks shipped from who-knows-where (though she prefers orchids), to find a husband already engrossed in the day's news and menu, in the next round of visitors, the next batch of mail.

Deep down, she knows she could have had more of his love if she could have given him more of hers. But she also knows that her supply of love is limited, and he is insatiable, like the mill downriver that needs constant water. No matter how much she gives him, he will want more from her—and still more from others. She sometimes feels like she is just one of many tributaries powering him. And if she gives him her love and he still needs more from others, she will dry up completely. *Love the kind you long for*, he had once promised her.

And so she marks this fortieth wedding anniversary now, to herself. "Congratulations," she says but her words are swallowed by the waterfall noise outside. "On your accomplishment."

She has no idea what she means.

The warmth of this first day of summer creeps into her room, and she decides to delay her arrival downstairs by taking a cold shower. As she steps out of her clothes and into the shower, she imagines she is stepping under a waterfall.

FLLW

Disintegrated by temperatures, ground down by glaciers, eroded by wind and sea, sculptured by timeless forces. Continually changed by cosmic forces themselves a form of change.

LILIANE

"Phillip, send for Florence, would you please?"

Liliane and her friend Tillie are poolside up at the guesthouse. Phillip has just served two tall glasses of carbonated water poured over a new French liqueur Liliane learned about in California, where her husband is now. He has built another house by another architect. He can't even remain faithful to an architect. The pink drinks fizz atop the ice cubes, and each glass is adorned with an orange pansy. It is the fourth such drink Phillip has served them, and Liliane's words begin to cascade from her mouth.

"Do you see, Tillie, how I call on one person to get another person. How this person does this job and the other does that? Phillip's job is to bring us refills and to find Florence. Florence's job is to listen to me. And to say the things I want to hear. Of course we call her job something else on paper, and I give her other tasks, don't get me wrong—oh fine, here she comes now—but sometimes it's lonely here with all these trees."

Tillie takes a sip from her new drink and says the drinks just keep getting better.

"It's good to have you here," Liliane says. "I can talk to you, too."

"About what?"

"Anything, of course. Hello, Florence! Won't you sit with us? Oh, I should have had Phillip bring you a drink. Wouldn't that be something if I asked you to go get Phillip to bring you a drink? No, no. Here, have mine. I haven't started it yet."

"That's alright, Mrs. Kaufmann, I don't need a drink."

"Go on, Florence, take it."

"I just had a glass of water, Mrs. Kaufmann."

"It's okay, Liliane, you keep it," Tillie says.

"You know, he's thinking of selling the store," Liliane says. "A merger, he calls it." One of the dogs hops into Liliane's lap. She strokes its long hair and talks into its ear. "What do you think of that, little Pepe?"

"Mrs. Kaufmann, may I—"

"Florence, how many women would you say he has had here? Five? Ten?"

Florence rises, shaking her head.

"Florence, I need a figure. Tillie here is going to make a commemorative sculpture. One for each of his women."

Liliane takes a long drink. In fact, it is not the quantity of women that bothers her now. It is this new one and the way it feels different. Her husband with his letters and his I remembers. Her Edgar with his new nurse.

"Liliane, maybe Florence has some work she needs to finish doing. Why don't we finish talking about my sculpture I was telling you about. It has nothing to do with E.J."

"Florence," says Liliane, "is a lovely city. I sat for a portrait there once."

LILIANE

The man from the *Pittsburgh Gazette* will arrive any minute and behind all of his questions about the chic apartment, their elegant lifestyle, and her volunteer work will be the questions he will not ask—will not need to ask—because he already knows the answers. Most likely he knows more than she, and the temptation will be for her to interview him. *Tell me,* she will want to ask, *how serious is it, this thing with the nurse?*

The journalist, if that's what you could call him, requested that she wear her Red Cross Nurse's Aid uniform, a symbolic gesture. "Personal interest," he explained. Liliane has obliged even though she would much rather wear one of the new dresses that had just arrived at the store from Paris, something that would match the interior décor of the European-styled apartment a bit better. She has obliged as a reminder that she too is a goddamn nurse.

The bell rings, the dog leaps off her lap, and the butler calls. Liliane rises, brushes stray hairs from her skirt, and welcomes the journalist with her warmest smile. She sits for photos, endures the questions, and withholds her own. Afterward she is spent.

She cannot know that decades later the same journalist will enter this very apartment to interview a new lady of the house, whom he will describe as the "dark-eyed vivacious" Mrs. Boonisar. "Former Edgar Kaufmann Room Gets Décor," the article will say, ten years after Liliane and Edgar are both gone. In the article, Liliane will be referred to as the "first Mrs. Kaufmann."

She cannot know these things, yet somehow they weigh on her. Tonight, alone in the city, is blight. Tomorrow she will go to Bear Run, and she is glad. Glad for the movement (else she might never leave bed), glad for the role she will play (to be driven, waited upon), glad for the water and its rush and sound. In the city there is noise, but it is white noise, synthetic like the music they have installed in the elevators. At Bear Run it is white water, *ahi opihǝle*, ancient and alive.

LILIANE

It was not entirely clear which came first: the nurse or the need for one. Had her husband's body flared with pains and pangs before or after he found a Stoop to soothe them?

Nor was it clear now whether Liliane first saw or simply sensed—like a wolf—the skirted silhouette of a smoking, smiling, straddled Stoops in her Bear Run living room. Regardless, the image burns in Liliane's mind like an undeveloped negative: the black picture window, white lips, black teeth, white eyes, black hair.

The freshly lit cigarette is not lost on Liliane. They would have heard Liliane's car arrive. Surely the staff communicated with one another, anticipating this moment. So, they had elected not to tell Mr. K—. All the better to snicker and sneer at the boss's moment of capture. The cigarette, then, had been lit in the moment of anticipation. Upon hearing her car, Liliane's husband, having nowhere to hide, would have risen and extended the flame. Stoops would have leaned forward, gazed into his eyes, drawn in deeply, and then slouched back, straddled, smug.

Let her Stoop in any of the other houses. Not this one.

Liliane stands in the middle of the room and studies the tableaux before her, still a black and white negative, and imagines exposing the image to light, burning and erasing it. No one speaks; Stoops draws another toke of the cigarette. The waterfall thunders its *sturm und drang* through the open balcony doors, and Liliane imagines her own mouth, open, with the waterfall as the voice of her fury.

She gathers her wits and does what she has learned, over the years, over the decades, to do. She pulls rank.

"When you're off duty, Nurse, do have Edgar make you a margarita. His are divine." She drops her bags on the ground and presses her palm forcefully on her seated husband's shoulder—one of the pained points that Stoops is hired to fix—and says to him, "Go easy on the tequila, darling. She's such a wee thing." Liliane removes a cigarette from the open pack on the desk and leans her face toward her husband for a light. "In the meantime," she says, taking a seat near Stoops, "would you take a look at my foot? I think I'm developing a dreadful bunion."

"She's not on duty, Liliane." He doesn't have the decency to be embarrassed, to avoid eye contact. But she holds his gaze long enough to let him know what she herself has just realized: This is it.

"Oh, well," Liliane says. "Then Paul can take her back to town while the engine is still warm."

She takes a drag on the cigarette and blows the smoke in the direction of Stoops.

That night, alone in her room, she is disgusted to find herself crying. But what else can she do? *Alles hat ein Ende.*

DEAR FRANK

I feel sure that by now you will have seen Edgar and will have gathered that the house in Palm Springs will in no sense have anything to do with me. Edgar and I will never share a house. That also means that when he returns I must leave Fallingwater, which is a great sorrow to me.

Therefore I have spent the last few weekends motoring about the countryside and I believe I have found a lovely spot in which to build a small house for myself.

Nine

JANIE

When Janie opens her eyes, the first thing she sees is a pinkish mound of mouth surrounded by pixels of gray and brown hair. Then she feels the mouth and coarse hair press on her forehead, moist heat expel from the nostrils onto her hairline, and a clamping pressure on each shoulder.

They are still on the famous balcony that juts out as far as physics should allow, that weighs so heavily on the floor below. The tour guide had described the work that had to be done to hold up the wings of the House. Gravity pushed down, and the Western Pennsylvania Conservancy pushed back up. It was worth it, of course, because the House is a national, historical, architectural treasure. She is not. Her marriage is not.

Janie knows enough to apologize as she shakes her head and says: "No. No, I can't, Andrew. We can't. I don't. I don't want a baby." She knows enough to look him in the eyes and say, "I'm sorry, Andrew. I'm so sorry," as they crumble under the weight of gravity.

THE DAUGHTER

Don't be sorry. It's just that I'm very tired. May I wake up now, Liliane?

Thank you.

AMANDA

What is the opposite of falling? Here at the southeast edge of Mrs. K—'s balcony, she can see the falling water, practically feel its spray. Maybe landing is the opposite of falling. Landing and getting back up, as she did at the door when the girl toppled her. She fell, landed, met the motorcycle man face to face, and she got back up.

She was toppled by her dad's death. Almost a year ago now. And she has spent the year falling. Following is what she usually does. Following rules, following schedules. But the rules broke, and her dad died. Her dad died and there was David, who felt fine.

The logic of her life had been confounded and she had embraced the confounded logic of David. But David's logic no longer made sense. People should answer their phones, return calls, be where they say they will be.

If I could, baby, I'd give you my world. Not that it was all his fault. He never asked for her world. *How can I, when you won't take it from me?*

Maybe when she made this weekend's plans she had landed. Even when David wasn't there, she had stuck to her plan. She showed up at the sport shop yesterday and signed her life away to raft through the white waters of the Youghiogheny River. The Yough, the guides called it—a sound between Yauk and Yog—full of familiarity and affection.

She was lined up with a group of fifty or so others at the river's edge to get helmets, life jackets, and paddles. Two yellow school buses exhaled diesel air. The young but seasoned guides strutted and lectured about the Lower Yough, the Middle Yough, the helmet strap, the proper way to hold a paddle.

"Now you need to find your groups! No more than six to a boat! When you have your group you need to pick a leader! That leader will follow my lead! Got it? The leader will tell you to paddle left or paddle right! Forward or back! Slow or fast!"

Amanda glanced around for a potential group.

"The Yough is higher than usual today! Do you know what that means?"

It had sounded menacing the way each monosyllable required its own shout.

"It means fast water!"

A group that had assembled near her seemed to have extra space. "Can I join you?" she said. Now she had to talk and smile and say where she was from.

"Sure, do you have anyone else with you?" they asked, counting heads.

"Yes," she heard herself say. "My dad." And when they didn't doubt her, she added, "But he didn't want to go rafting. Sprained ankle."

The group nodded. "Too bad," they said.

And just like that she had brought him back to life.

An hour or so later she was in her raft, tired but so far pleased to have made it with her group through Cucumber Rapids, Camel and Walrus Rapids, Eddy Turn, and Railroad Rapids. Each rapid was held breath, anxious paddling ("Right side, forward! Left side, back!" their chosen leader called), and strained muscles, followed by relief as the water carried them through a smooth stretch.

Now they were approaching Dimple Rock. They were told it was the most dangerous point of the course. They were not told that people had died there, though Amanda could sense it and would read about it later. The guides were getting out of their kayaks and positioning themselves on the shore, pointing toward Dimple Rock, saying this is your last chance to skip it, to get out and meet your raft downstream. Other guides were already setting up rescue gear. Amanda looked around: What to do?

One guide began shouting instructions again: "Listen up! You must take Dimple Rock at an angle to the right! After you pass Dimple Rock you must paddle hard left to avoid Pinball Rock! Does anyone want to guess why it's called Pinball? That's right! And your raft is the pinball!"

Amanda knew that this was why they had made her sign over her life. This was when she would have liked to have turned toward David and, with a nod and a smile, agreed that they would do this together, that they would be okay. And this was when it began to stir and swirl like river water around a rock: her fury. As the guide released one boat at a time toward Dimple Rock, as Amanda waited with her raftmates like a racehorse in the gate, she became aware of how wrong and how wronged she had been.

It was her raft's turn.

A guide on the rock to the left called out that they were doing great, right side paddle, well done, keep going, and then another guide on the right told them to do the opposite, still doing great, nice job, that's it, and then the river got louder, the raft got faster, and the guides got wilder, waving their arms, *that way, 1-1-8, that way!* As her group twirled and paddled and fought the currents she could tell that the river was a hungry beast: Dimple Rock and the other rocks were like teeth; the swirling waters an open mouth ready to swallow. The raft was turned to the right, positioned sideways, and headed straight for the rock with Amanda's side leading. *Left forward, 1-1-8, right back!* But the current was stronger than their paddles and the next thing she knew, her boat slammed into the rock, catapulting her into the churning waters. Even though she was in her body being bumped and cut by rocks, she felt bodiless, like a spirit, like Dad, released to die. When she knew she would not die and she was pulled back into the raft, the pain flaring in her body, she felt the fullness of her fury.

She is not sure she has ever been this sore in her life—her back muscles especially, and her bruised legs—but she is no longer falling. Below her is the top of the waterfall that drops over the broken rock edge. She is no longer following either. She will go her own way.

IRENE

I can't stop thinking of him. In my mind I see him motoring around PA, and the next thing I know I'm picturing myself wearing a helmet in one of those little sidecars with my name airbrushed on the side, riding along with him. And we're headed to the house built on the waterfall, like a couple might do. That's the danger, though, how you can create this whole unreal image of a person when he's not around, and then he returns and can't live up to what you've created out of the brick and mortar of your hopes and dreams. I'm so tired of asshole men, of being alone, so damn tired. I wasn't even going to go to the bar that night, and I just happened to turn into the gravel lot in the interest of delaying an appointment with the evening news. And what if I hadn't?

When Josiah gets back I'm going to apologize for calling him short all those weeks ago, and then we're going to go shopping for a sidecar.

THE DAUGHTER

The daughter opens her eyes and sees the upside down face of a ponytail man. His bright blue eyes are surrounded by blue-gray skies. She thinks of heaven. *Vom Himmel kommt es, Zum Himmel steigt es.* Huh?

"Oh, Melissa, thank God! Oh, honey!" She hears familiar voices but can't quite place them, feels eager squeezing of her arms.

"It might be good to give her just a minute," the ponytail man says, and the daughter is grateful. "You okay?" he asks her.

The daughter is not sure if she's okay. She's not sure where she is or has been. She hears only the song of the spirits over the waters.

AMANDA

The roar of the waterfall is like the fury of Dimple Rock and thank god David did not come. She would, by this moment, have come to this same conclusion if David were standing beside her rather than standing her up. But if he were here now, she would have to rid herself of him.

There is commotion behind her and the girl seems to have recovered. Even the Vikings look relieved.

From this balcony, she can see her past and her future. She peers over the ledge to the terrace directly below, where the Buddha head remains on its pedestal. A new group of tourists slowly circles it. That is her past.

Just above her to the right is another terrace, one she has not yet visited, where the top halves of another group seem to float. She meets eyes with one of the tourists—someone who also seems to be alone, someone from her future—and he does not, like the others, look away.

In fact, he smiles at her. She smiles back.

Ten

LILIANE

Oh, where is it? She knows it's here because this is its home. Of all the houses, this was the one where she kept Goethe. Goethe's words, Bear Run's waters, the architect's house, and Liliane herself: a family. When she was twelve, she found the poem, wrote the words, set her destiny in motion. Now she can't find the poem. There are the pills—she'll have another. The Virgin's eyes are like little pills. The water finally spoke to her, told her to get the poem. The books are all in a row on the stone hearth, but which one is Goethe? She touches her fingers to the spines just like she did all those years ago in Father's library. *Oh, Vater. Oh, Wasser.* And there he is, *Vater's* favorite: Goethe.

Even though she expects to see it, is in fact looking for it, it is a shock to hold the delicate paper, to see the words penned in her twelve-year-old hand, these fifty years hence. She sees in the small loops and long tails of her letters a hint of her present writing, the way she sometimes sees a glimpse of her aged self in old photographs, and vice versa. Had Edgar been there that day? The day she translated the poem? Why does it make her think of him?

Believe me when I say I love you more much more than any woman in the world.

Love the kind you long for.

Suddenly the pain comes again, like a violent waterfall: Stoops.

What's that? The water is talking to her again. It is giving her a message.

The water is correct: Stoops is not even as old as the paper in Liliane's hands! There had been no Stoops in the world then. Only Liliane. She had still been Lillian. Somehow this makes her hurt again. The shapes of the letters on the fragile paper twist inside her. She wants to talk to that young girl in her father's library and apologize for what happened to her. Isn't Liliane somehow responsible? But, then again, hadn't the girl loved her cousin, hadn't the girl wanted him no matter the price? Silly girl. *She* should apologize to Liliane, who has spent her life paying and paying.

No, she is confused again.

The water speaks to her again, instructs Liliane to get into bed. With effort, she obliges. Whether it is the water or her own voice that says, *Des Menschen Seele Gleicht dem Wasser: Vom Himmel kommt es, Zum Himmel steigt es,* she does not know.

JUNIOR

will say that his mother committed suicide, that she died at Fallingwater. She will be found unconscious in her room, but pronounced dead two hours away in Pittsburgh after Edgar gambles on superior doctors over precious time—and loses. The coroner's results will be inconclusive as to whether her overdose was accidental or—

FLLW

The truth is more important than the facts.

STOOPS

will be the hostess of the funeral and will marry the widower and when he dies she will sue for his estate and

(these are the facts)

will lose

will develop multiple sclerosis by age forty

will be alone in her apartment in her wheelchair one night when her heating pad catches fire

and (this is the truth)

will die fifteen minutes before her maid arrives.

SONG OF THE SPIRITS OVER THE WATERS

Soul of man,
How you resemble the water!
Fate of man,
How you resemble the wind!

LETTER FROM EDGAR

My Dearest Love: —

If this reaches you and finds you lonely or bewildered or sorrowful—if my arms cannot make themselves felt about you, if I seem lost to you—remember that you need only go alone a little way farther ... that at any unexpected corner we may come face to face, heart to heart; that the present is only a veil for the future; and that far beyond eternity I love you.

Edgar

JUNIOR

will relocate his mother's body and bury his parents together at Fallingwater. Years later he will have his own ashes scattered on its grounds and in its waters.

SONG OF THE SPIRITS
OVER THE WATERS

And in the waveless lake
All the stars
Feast on their likeness.

DEAR JUNIOR

Your mother needs no sympathy.
She shines brighter now that she no longer suffers.

—*Frank Lloyd Wright*

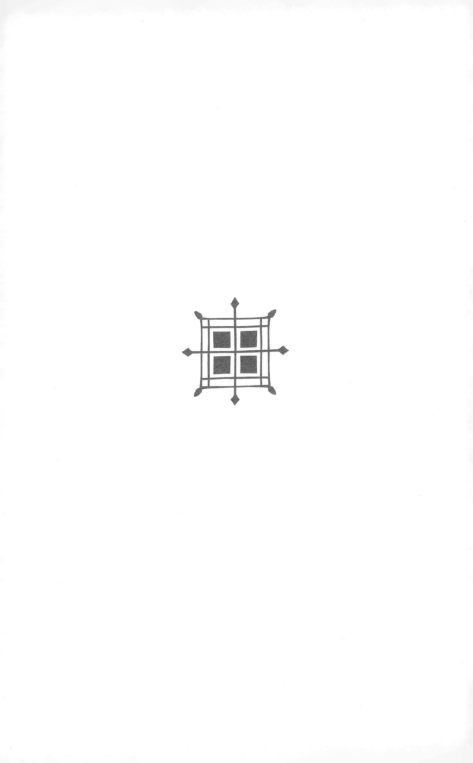

AUTHOR'S NOTE

My own Fallingwater story began in 2009 when I spent a few days in Ohiopyle, Pennsylvania, with my family and we decided to take a tour on our way out of town. By the time the tour was over, I knew two things: I had to write about this place, and the story would be a domestic tragedy. What I did not know was that a domestic tragedy had already occurred there. Franklin Toker's *Fallingwater Rising* first introduced me to the dynamics of the Kaufmann marriage, and I was captivated by the submerged story of Liliane Kaufmann. I drew upon Toker's book to imagine key events—including Liliane's portrait session with Victor Hammer, her encounter with Frida Kahlo, and her death—as well as for the architectural and metaphorical significance of Liliane's balcony. Though I made up the character of Richard, Toker suggests that Liliane likely had other lovers.

Neil Levine's discussion of "The Temporal Dimension of Fallingwater" in *The Architecture of Frank Lloyd Wright* further informed this book's shape and themes. The multiple voices and hybrid structure emerged in the earliest draft, and I came to see the form as analogous to that of Fallingwater. Just as Fallingwater's stone chimney serves as the structure's vertical core, rising from the rock foundation and supporting the rest of the house, Liliane's story serves as this book's core. The other characters' sections extend forth like multiple cantilevered balconies. I also knew very early on that the book would be a novella—that Fallingwater is, to my mind, a novella-sized house.

My research also led me to the serendipitous discovery of Liliane Kaufmann's personal letters at the Jacob Rader Marcus Center of the American Jewish Archives in Cincinnati, Ohio, in a building that I had walked past twice a day from my nearby apartment to graduate school at the University of Cincinnati from 2000 to 2006. The bulk of the letters are from Edgar when he was stationed at Camp Taylor in Kentucky during World War I, and they reveal a side of Edgar and Liliane's relationship that is, to me, more intimate than expected and thus more heartbreaking. I've used a number of excerpts from the letters in the manuscript; all the Edgar sections are his actual words.

Since my first trip to Fallingwater, I have returned many times as both a tourist and, in 2012, as a volunteer Ask-Me Guide. I am struck again and again by the way Fallingwater is not just an architectural wonder, but a communal source of stories.

—*Kelcey Parker*

SOURCES

I have taken some liberties with the story of Liliane Kaufmann, but the foundation of her story, as well as the actual correspondence and direct quotes from Frank Lloyd Wright (appearing within as FLLW), are drawn from the following:

Cleary, Richard L. *Merchant Prince and Master Builder: Edgar J. Kaufmann and Frank Lloyd Wright*. Seattle: U of Washington P, 1999.

Futagawa, Yukio, ed. *Frank Lloyd Wright: Fallingwater*. Tokyo: A.D.A. EDITA, 2003.

Gray, Kevin. "Modern Gothic." *NYT Magazine* 23 Sept. 2001.

Harris, Leon. *Merchant Princes: An Intimate History of Jewish Families Who Built Great Department Stores*. New York: Berkley, 1979.

Hoffmann, Donald. *Frank Lloyd Wright's Fallingwater: The House and Its History*. New York: Dover, 1993.

Huxtable, Ada Louise. *Frank Lloyd Wright: A Life*. New York: Penguin, 2004.

Kaufmann, Edgar, jr. *Fallingwater: A Frank Lloyd Wright Country House*. New York: Abbeville, 1986.

Levine, Neil. *The Architecture of Frank Lloyd Wright*. Princeton, NJ: Princeton UP, 1996.

Martinson, Suzanne. *The Fallingwater Cookbook: Elsie Henderson's Recipes and Memories*. Pittsburgh: U of Pittsburgh P, 2008.

Toker, Franklin. *Fallingwater Rising: Frank Lloyd Wright, E.J. Kaufmann, and America's Most Extraordinary House*. New York: Knopf, 2005.

Waggoner, Linda, ed. *Fallingwater*. New York: Rizzoli, 2011.

Walker, Frances. "Former Edgar Kaufmann Room Gets Décor." *Pittsburgh Post-Gazette* 26 Oct. 1966: 19.

Wright, Frank Lloyd. *Modern Architecture: Being the Kahn Lectures for 1930*. 1931. Princeton: Princeton UP, 2008.

—. *The Essential Frank Lloyd Wright: Critical Writings on Architecture*. Ed. Bruce Brooks Pfeiffer. Princeton: Princeton UP, 2008.

—. *A Testament*. New York: Horizon, 1957.

—. *An Autobiography*. 1943. San Francisco: Pomegranate, 2005.

Other direct quotations throughout the book are from the following:

The "Edgar Remembers" and "Letter from Edgar" sections are transcriptions of actual letters from Edgar Kaufmann to Liliane Kaufmann held in the Kaufmann Collection, SC-1506, at the Jacob Rader Marcus Center of the American Jewish Archives, Cincinnati, Ohio.

The original German version of Johann Wolfgang von Goethe's 1779 poem, *"Gesang der Geister über den Wassern"* is from *Introduction to German Poetry: A Dual-Language Book*, edited by Gustave Mathieu and Guy Stern and published in 1987 by Dover, New York.

The English translation of Johann Wolfgang von Goethe's poem, *"Gesang der Geister über den Wassern"* is ©2003 by Shawn Thuris, hosted at www.recmusic.org/lieder.

The song lyrics listed in the Amanda sections are from "Go Your Own Way," written by Lindsey Buckingham, performed by Fleetwood Mac on the 1977 album *Rumours*, released by Warner Bros. Records. (Note: Some quotes are intentionally incorrect interpretations of the lyrics.)

The song lyrics listed on page 114 are from "It's the End of the World as We Know It (And I Feel Fine)," written by R.E.M. and recorded on the 1987 album *Document*, released by I.R.S. Records.

ACKNOWLEDGMENTS

I wish to extend my deepest thanks to Abigail Beckel and Kathleen Rooney of Rose Metal Press for seeing promise in the original manuscript and for helping it find its final form. At Fallingwater I met so many wonderful staff members and volunteers, and I'm especially grateful to Jennifer Hiebert and Amy Humbert, who welcomed me as the volunteer with the longest commute. Thanks to Lowell Britson for wonderful chats at AWP. Thanks to Elisa Ho, associate archivist at the Jacob Rader Marcus Center of the American Jewish Archives, for her help in accessing the Kaufmann letters.

Thanks also to Martha Nichols, editor of *Talking Writing*, where the opening prologue was originally published in September 2010, and to Steve Himmer, editor of *Necessary Fiction*, where a "Janie" excerpt was published in July 2012.

Thanks to Caitlin Horrocks, Jim Daniels, Chris Bachelder, and Cathy Day for the kind words. And thanks to Michael

Griffith for not only the kind words but also the many years of mentorship and support.

Finally, thanks to my beloved family and friends—near and far, living and gone. Especially to Janice Bobrovcan, Gary and Pat Ervick, Darcy Ervick; Dane, Melissa, Xander, and Lachlann Ervick; and Christian and Travis Ervick. To B.J. and Monte Parker. In memory of my grandparents, John and Margaret Bobrovcan. And in memory of Lukas Scott Wilson, my first love, my ghost.

ABOUT THE AUTHOR

Kelcey Parker's first book, *For Sale By Owner* (Kore Press), won the 2011 Next Generation Indie Book Award in Short Fiction and was a Finalist for the 2012 Best Books of Indiana. She directs the creative writing program at Indiana University South Bend. During the summer of 2012, she worked as an Ask-Me Guide at Fallingwater, where she asked as many questions as she answered, helped visitors get the perfect photo of Fallingwater, and always kept an eye out for Liliane's ghost.

A NOTE ABOUT THE TYPE

The main text of *Liliane's Balcony* is set in Electra, which was designed for Linotype by W. A. Dwiggins in 1935, the same year Frank Lloyd Wright designed Fallingwater. Of Electra, Dwiggins said, "I'd like to make it warm, so full of blood and personality that it would jump at you." With the typeface's streamlined curves and exceptional legibility, it has become a popular book type that well accomplishes Dwiggins' goal.

DTL Nobel is used both for the title on the cover and as a display face throughout the interior. It was designed by Sjoerd Hendrik de Roos and Dick Dooijes in the early 1930s for the Amsterdam Type Foundry in Lettergieterij Amsterdam, and was inspired by the popularity that Futura was experiencing during that period. In 1993 Nobel was revived simultaneously by the Dutch Type Library under the designers Andrea Fuchs and Fred Smeijers, and by Font Bureau under Tobias Frere-Jones. More organic than other geometric sans serifs, Nobel has a strong mid-twentieth century undercurrent.

The secondary cover typeface is Eaglefeather, which is based on the alphabet Frank Lloyd Wright designed in 1922 for his Eagle Rock project. It was created by David Siegel in 1996.

Ornaments from the P22 FLLW Terra Extras collection, designed by Frank Lloyd Wright, are also used throughout the interior—most notably under the character names in the section openers and in the folios.

—Heather Butterfield